A REALLY AWESOME MESS

A REALLY AWESOME MESS

TRISH COOK AND BRENDAN HALPIN

EGMONT
USA
NEW YORK

EGMONT

We bring stories to life

First published by Egmont USA, 2013
443 Park Avenue South, Suite 806
New York, NY 10016
Copyright © Trish Cook and Brendan Halpin, 2013
All rights reserved
1 3 5 7 9 8 6 4 2
www.egmontusa.com
www.trishcook.com
www.brendanhalpin.com
Library of Congress Cataloging-in-Publication Data

Cook, Trish, 1965- author.
A really awesome mess / Trish Cook and Brendan Halpin.
pages cm
Summary: An angry girl and a depressed boy, both sixteen, are sent to a therapeutic boarding school.
ISBN 978-1-60684-363-5 (hardcover) -- ISBN 978-1-60684-364-2 (ebook)
[1. Emotional problems--Fiction. 2. Psychotherapy--Fiction. 3. Chinese Americans--Fiction. 4. Boarding schools--Fiction. 5. Schools--Fiction.] I. Halpin, Brendan, 1968- author. II. Title.
PZ7.C773Re 2013   [Fic]--dc23
                                    2012045978

Printed in the United States of America

Book Design by Torborg Davern

To Courtney and Kelsey, who light up my life.

—T.C.

If you're getting through high school with anxiety and depression on board, I dedicate this book to you.

—B.H.

A REALLY AWESOME MESS

I.

EMMY

"HOME CRAPPY HOME," I WHISPERED UNDER MY BREATH.

Dropping my duffel bag on the worn hardwood floor, I scanned the claustrophobic room. Above me: A low, oddly angled ceiling that made the cramped space feel like it might swallow me whole. Straight ahead: A tall, skinny window with bars on the outside, presumably so I wouldn't a) fall or b) hurl myself out of it, flanked by plain wooden dressers. To my right: Twin beds crammed into an L-shape, each with a big-ass bulletin board hanging above it. Pee-yellow walls all around.

The already-claimed mattress was covered in a barn red comforter and had a big stuffed pig on top of it. Farm Girl—which was what I'd already nicknamed my new roommate in my head, and hoped wouldn't actually come out of my mouth when I met her—had plastered every last inch of her board in cutesy animal pictures and 4-H ribbons. The bed and board meant for me, of course, were still naked.

"Heartland Academy is going to be such a great experience for you, Emmy," my mom said, a fake smile glued to her face. "Take it all in. Give it everything you've got!"

I couldn't believe she was pulling out an inspirational speech at a time like this. It would have been more honest if she'd just crowed, "Later, sucker!" and hightailed out of there never to return, because the truth of the matter was inescapable. She and Dad were finally getting rid of me. I mean, Dad hadn't even bothered to come to drop me off here, claiming he didn't have any more vacations days left after all the meetings at school and with the police and whoever else had gotten pissed at me recently.

I also knew the lame excuse the 'rents were using—*We need you to learn to be healthy again, both mentally and physically*—wasn't the real reason they were sending me away. Reality: Despite the twenty pounds I'd lost recently, I was still the elephant in the room. Though we'd all tried our best to deny it, I was always going to be a living, breathing reminder of my parents' painful bout with infertility. Lucky for them, the infertility had turned out to be temporary and they'd ended up making a kid the old-fashioned way. Unlucky for me, they now wanted to cut bait on the sole vestige of a very sad time in their lives.

"Yeah, totes. This place seems really chill, Em," my little sister Jocelyn piped in, checking out a picture of a hedgehog wearing a daisy-print hat on Farm Girl's bulletin board.

The "little" in little sister would be a relative term here. For pretty much our whole lives, Joss has towered over me. Other things, in addition to tall, that Joss is and I am not: Fair-skinned, blond, and freckled. Athletic. Biologically related to my mom and dad.

I stared around the room, then back at Joss again. She couldn't be serious.

"I guess what I meant was, I'm sure it'll be way better than the Internet made it out to be," she qualified, wincing.

We'd spent the last few days holed up in my room, poring over the Heartland Academy and Rate My School websites, looking for clues as to what my daily life might be like here and how long my involuntary admission might last. Heartland's made it look a lot like summer camp—arts and crafts, ropes courses, trust games, that kind of stuff—with regular classes and tons of psychotherapy thrown in; Rate My School's assessment probably cut a lot closer to the truth. *Hell in a cornfield*, *Pointless and stupid*, and *Jail* were just a few of the descriptors former students had posted anonymously. And after the long, bleak orientation I'd just sat through with the other new kids who for the most part looked like total freaks, I was even more inclined to agree with the Rate My Schoolies.

"You want to stay here in my place?" I joked with Joss.

I was only half kidding. Joss had been known to do other heroic things for me, like beating up the mean boy in preschool who said we couldn't be sisters because I was a "ching chong bing bong." Like inviting me along to parties and dances with her friends because the few I had tended to be socially awkward and anxious. Like choosing to stay home with me instead of hitting those same parties and dances after the shit flew and even my socially awkward and anxious friends deserted me.

Tears pooled in Joss's eyes. "I wish I could," she said, sniffling. "Really I do."

Mom decided Joss needed defending, which was ridiculous because we weren't even fighting. I couldn't remember us *ever* really fighting. "It is not Jocelyn's responsibility to rescue you from this situation. Nor is it mine or your dad's. You'll have to do that for yourself this time."

She sounded just like the parents' section of the Heartland website. I wondered if they'd made her memorize lines like that during her orientation, and that's why it had been held separately from mine.

"Things really got blown out of proportion, don't you think?" I said, staring down at my feet and scrunching up my toes in my kid-sized Converse.

Mom answered my question with another question. "You're surprised that parents, your school, and the police take bullying—especially when it is carried out online for everyone to see—seriously?"

I sighed heavily. "Mom, I told you a million times, I posted those things on Facebook in self-defense. Danny Schwartz bullied me first!"

"Then perhaps you should have reported him to the school administrators rather than taking matters into your own hands, Emmy," my mom said. Her eyes kept darting toward the door, like she was plotting her escape from me even as we spoke.

I took some slow, deliberate breaths—another dumbass thing suggested on the Heartland website—to try and keep my head from exploding off my body. What my mom didn't know (and what I'd never tell her) was I couldn't have reported that douche Danny—who liked to sing *me so horny* every time he saw me in the halls—no matter how much I wanted to. And here's why: According to the rules of my swanky private school, we would have then been obligated to have our argument mediated.

Which would have meant talking about what had prompted his racist, sexist remarks.

In front of a bunch of student mediators and teachers overseeing the proceedings.

Sure, they might have made Danny apologize even if he refused to admit what he'd done. But his fake apology wasn't worth me having to expose myself any further than I already had. And I was positive that asshole would have found a way to work the mortifying reason he was harassing me in the first place into the conversation.

So narcing on him had never even been a remote possibility in my mind. Instead, I launched an online counterattack meant to publicly humiliate the guy the way he was publicly humiliating me. Over the course of five days, I spammed choice words and photos disparaging him all over FB. One of my favorites: *Dan Schwartz has the genitals of a Girl Scout*, accompanied by a picture of a half-eaten Samoa cookie. I thought it was pretty funny, especially since word at school was the guy had a total chode in his pants.

Even funnier, that particular post had gotten 256 likes. Which, of course, Danny didn't like at all. So he screenshotted all my little digs and reported me to his parents, who in turn reported me to the school, who in turn reported me to the local police.

The power trio was not amused in the least bit. I got grounded for an undetermined amount of time that still hadn't ended, not that I cared to go out anyhow; a lecture from Officer Friendly about online etiquette that wrapped up with a fifteen-hour community service sentence, which I kind of liked because speed-shelving books at the library turned out to be great cardio; and a week-long suspension from school that came as a welcome relief because I could barely get myself out of bed and dressed in the morning, I was so stressed by that point.

I was told I could return to school once seven days was up and I issued an apology to *me so horny*-singing Danny Schwartz. Naturally, I declined. So then they declined to let me back in.

My parents, baffled by my uncharacteristic mean behavior and subsequent stubbornness, begged and pleaded with me to apologize. Even Joss, who knew why I'd gone after Danny Schwartz like a rabid pit bull, advised me to just suck it up so I could get out of trouble. But there was no way—not a chance in hell, not then, not now, not ever—he was going to hear the words *I'm sorry* pass my lips. No f-ing way.

It turned into a total standoff, which left me in quite the quandry, school-wise. Since all this happened with only three weeks left of the academic year, my by now totally freaked out parents convinced the powers that be to let me complete the rest of my assignments and take finals from home. I was like, halle-freaking-lujah, because it meant I wouldn't have to put up with people staring at me and whispering about me in the halls anymore.

I assumed I'd spend the entire summer much in the same way as the end of the academic year—hanging out with my sister or in my room on my computer—and then head off someplace else in the fall. Though the public school was the most likely suspect, what I really wanted to do was get the hell out of dodge and start over somewhere else. During one of my long, boring afternoons spent online, I'd discovered this cool place called Bard College at Simon's Rock. It offered an "early college program," admitting students right after sophomore year—like I'd just finished—and letting them skip the rest of high school and start college right away. It seemed tailor-made for smart kids like me who couldn't stand one more second of bitchy cliques and immature, judgmental classmates. I was *dying* to go there.

But then my parents decided I was too "fragile" or something to handle the change. To the highly selective, faraway-from-home Simon's Rock *or* the mediocre local public high school. *Not pleased* doesn't begin to describe my reaction.

The fragile thing, I knew, was just another excuse. I might have been small—granted, much smaller than I used to be, back when I looked like a bloated blueberry next to my celery stalk family—but that didn't mean I wasn't strong. What other five-foot-nothing, now-ninety-pound girl could have taken down a big bad Danny Schwartz and stuck to her guns even after he went crying to his mommy and the principal and Officer Friendly?

"The point is, you're the one who got yourself into such trouble at Stonebridge Country Day," my mom said. "If you'd just apologized to Daniel, the school would have let you come back for your junior year—"

I shook my head furiously. "No. Never! I would rather be stuck in this hellhole until I turn eighteen."

"Which you just might be," my mom said, her palms upward

like *Your choice, kiddo. It's out of my hands now. I'm letting you go.*

I felt hot tears in the corners of my eyes, but I was damned if they were going to fall. "Well then. I guess you got what you wanted, and I got what I deserved, huh?"

This, of course, made my mom turn on the waterworks I was busy holding in. "Do you honestly think this is how we want things to be, Emmy? We're going to miss you so much. I'm already dreaming of the day my beautiful star is healthy enough to come home."

Right. The "beautiful star" crap again. It was what my real name—my Chinese name—meant. My parents had been telling me the same bullshit story for as far back as I could remember: *We saw a beautiful star in the sky and it was you, calling us to China to come get you. We were all meant to be together.* Well, maybe that had been true for all of about a week. And then they found out Joss had somehow implanted herself in my mom's supposedly defective uterus.

Too bad my parents had already told everyone about me, or they probably would've just left me stranded at that orphanage for some other suckers to adopt. But things being the way they were, the 'rents were obligated to come get me or they would've looked like the world's biggest assholes. And that was why, instead of just having one tall, beautiful, blond biologically related kid, my parents got stuck raising a small, dark, chubby China doll, too.

The four of us made for a weird-looking family. There were three people who obviously fit together and one who obviously did not, like I was a piece of a different puzzle that had somehow made its way into the wrong box. To make matters worse, even though I was a full eleven months older than Joss, from age three or so on she'd always been the "bigger" sister. Or should I say, the taller and skinnier one. Which would, by default, make me the short, fat one.

All this led to a lifetime of awkward stares and stupid comments that were amplified times a million because we were in the same grade at school. "You must be twins, hahaha," went the most annoying "joke." "How does anyone tell you two apart?" My parents had always told us to laugh along with the less enlightened and tell them families were based on love, not looks. Joss had no problem following their advice; me, not so much. How other people viewed us cut me to the core every time. It felt like everyone knew my ugly secret—that my real family had gotten rid of me and this nice white one had taken pity on my poor orphaned self—and it left me feeling raw and exposed as a turtle without a shell.

The more I thought about the situation, the more pissed off I got. There had been so many other viable alternatives, but my parents had chosen the wrong ones every single time. And now they were acting like *I* was the one with the problem? It was all such bullshit. Had I asked to be born? Was it my fault my mom chose not to keep me? Did I somehow trick my parents into going ahead with the adoption?

I didn't think so.

"If I really was your beautiful star, I think you would've just let me go to Simon's Rock or even the stupid public high school instead of this loony bin," I hissed, surprised at how deeply I actually felt the venom I was spewing. "At least my real parents were honest about the reason they were ditching me—I had a vag, not a dick. You're just dumping me because I'm not a perfect blond Amazon like the rest of you."

Which made my mom put her face into her hands and sob. It was exactly what I wanted to do, to cry and beg her to take me home. I just kept quiet instead. I'd tried begging for a different outcome *a lot* in the last couple of days, and it hadn't gotten me anywhere. Ditto for yelling, screaming, and the silent treatment. I was too washed out and used up at this point to exert that kind of energy when I knew the end result would be the same. I was staying here, they were going home without me, and that was that.

A woman wearing a green Heartland Academy sweatshirt knocked on the open door and interrupted our lovely little pain festival. "Sorry. I've know you've seen me pop my head in the doorway a couple of times, Mrs. Magnusson. I was trying to wait until an opportune moment, but I guess this will have to do. You need to say good-bye now."

My mom walked over and wrapped me in her arms, hugging me so hard I thought I might burst. I let her hold me but didn't hug back, my arms hanging by my side like wet noodles. "I love you so much, sweetie," she whispered in my ear.

Yeah, right, I thought. *You love me so much you're leaving skid marks.*

When my mom finally let me go, Joss threw her arms around me. I clung to her like a baby monkey. "I promise I'll e-mail every day, sis," she whispered, her voice choked and small. The archaic means of communication was necessary, of course, because texts and phone calls and other normal ways of contacting someone weren't allowed at Heartland, at least not until I jumped through what sounded like a million hoops.

"Looking forward to seeing you again at the end of summer term for Family Weekend," the woman in the sweatshirt called after my mom and sister as they left my room. Then she turned and handed me a striped hospital gown. "I'll need you to get undressed and put this on, Mei-Xing."

She said it like this: *Meee-zing.*

I glared at her. "First of all, it's pronounced *May-shing*. Second of all, I go by Emmy, so don't ever call me that again. And third, I'm not carrying or packing, so I won't be needing this." I threw the gown back at her.

The woman just smiled and handed it to me again. "You'll get used to the rules here soon enough. And rule number one is that every time you come in from being off campus, you have to give us a urine sample and have a strip search."

"And if I don't do it?" I asked.

"I'm confident you'll make the right choice. Because let's face it—all the wrong choices are what landed you here in the first place. And I'd hazard a guess that what you want most right now is to go home. Following the rules is your quickest way back."

The lady was right. I was completely screwed, so I grabbed the pee cup and gown and did what I was told.

CHAPTER TWO

JUSTIN

ACETAMINOPHEN.

This is the word that should pretty much convince anybody it wasn't a serious suicide attempt. I mean, it's freaking Tylenol. We've got a three-story house. A header off the roof into the driveway would have finished me off way more efficiently than seventeen over-the-counter painkillers.

Which, as it turned out, would have finished me off in a pretty nasty way if I hadn't received medical intervention. Yeah, I've got Internet access like everybody else, so I could have looked it up, but I honestly didn't know. I figured, pop a few Tylenol just to put a scare into Mom, no big deal. Turns out the dose I took actually would have been fatal if I hadn't gotten the old stomach pump (inaccurately named, by the way. It was actually a stomach

14

vacuum. Like they literally snaked a tube down my throat and sucked out everything in my stomach. It would have been cool as hell if it were happening to somebody else).

And then some medicine to make sure my liver didn't shut down.

It wasn't a fun night for anybody, but, I mean, okay, classic cry for help, we'll deal with it in therapy.

But then I guess I was "acting out sexually." Apparently this is some kind of sign of adolescent mental health issues. But as far as I could tell from everybody I know, it is not acting out sexually that causes the mental health issues. Those kids with the "purity rings" at school? Those were some psychos. Me?

Well, I got flown out to Dad's house for Memorial Day weekend because Mom thought reconnecting with him and getting a change of scenery would help me. Those were her words, though I would not have used "reconnect," because it implied there had once been a connection. Mom left Dad when I was two and a half, and he hadn't been much of a dad since then, so if there ever was a connection, it was from before I remember, which means it didn't count, at least as far as I was concerned.

I guess Dad didn't really want to reconnect, or, actually, connect either. He bought me a weekend pass to King's Island, borrowed Aunt Meg's old Infiniti for me, and said he had a lot of work to catch up on, good to see you buddy.

Which was how I wound up acting out sexually. Getting a

blow job at Dad's house from a girl I'd just met at King's Island. After we rode The Beast. Write your own joke, and while you're doing that, I'll just remember . . . I think her name was Caitlin, but it could have been Kristin—something that ended in "in." So we rode The Beast together, just because we were both alone in line at the same time, and then I was like, let me buy you something fried and disgusting, and she was like cool, and then she was talking about her stupid boyfriend who she just dumped in the line for The Racer, and then she was like, oh crap, I don't have a ride home, and I was like, oh well, I've got my car here (it was, of course, my aunt Meg's car, but when you're sixteen and rollin' in an Infiniti, even an '04, you do not volunteer that it's not yours), let me give you a ride home.

And oh yeah, let me just stop by my dad's Rich Divorced Guy condo, and while we're here, you wanna make out? She did, and the next thing I knew, she was introducing me to the art of oral gratification. The next thing I knew after that, well before the event came to what should have been its rightful conclusion, my dad came home from work two hours early, which he'd never done before in his life, walked in and saw us on the couch, and shouted, "I'm not running a bordello here!"

A bordello. I had to look it up. The first definition I found said, "a house of ill repute," which wasn't much help. Basically he was calling Caitlin or Kristin a whore, which was a crappy thing to do because believe me, it wasn't like I had girls lining up to blow me, and she certainly wasn't demanding any payment. I would have liked to maybe see her again even though I only had a day left at Dad's house, but I guess him walking in pretty well killed the mood forever with Kitten or whatever the hell her name was. (Aside—if you're ever asked to go to the board in math class and you're stuck with one of those stubborn boners that won't go away, picturing your dad walking in on you is enough to make you go limp for hours. I had to take the equipment for a test-drive later that evening just to make sure everything had recovered from the shock. Also to relieve the horrible, nut-busting ache of blue balls that arises when your dad walks in before you get to finish your first blow job ever in proper fashion. Not that I'm bitter.)

That was Memorial Day weekend. Now it was just past the Fourth of July and I was being shipped off to a "therapeutic setting." Dad said he would pay for it and kind of insisted, after threatening to take Mom and Patrick to court for custody, which they couldn't afford. He'd decided they weren't doing enough to ensure my mental health, so he sent two registered letters to Mom and Patrick. Which was two more letters than I could ever remember him sending me.

And yeah, I was sure Mom and Patrick were happy to get rid of me anyway. They could focus on the twins, not have to bother with me, the Troubled One. Great. Dad's money solved another problem.

This was all the stuff I was thinking as we drove through miles and miles of nothing. Well, not nothing. There was a lot of corn, which I recognized, and some other shorter green stuff, which I didn't recognize.

There was a truck stop. And then some more corn. And a little more corn. And then, between two cornfields, a small road and a wooden sign that said, "Heartland Academy. A Caring Place."

We drove for at least two minutes on this little road before I saw Heartland Academy looming in the distance. It was an old, creepy-looking building. The windows were arched, the walls were stone, and there were acres and acres of short grass lawns surrounding it.

I guess it was pretty good proof against escape: Even if you got out of the building, you had to walk for several minutes across lawns with no cover. And once you did that, there was nothing but corn for miles and miles.

Slayer was in my earbuds screaming about the angel of death. I wasn't a huge metalhead or anything, but it just seemed kind of appropriate as we approached the place I was going to be spending the next . . . well, Mom and Patrick were a little unclear about the length of time. "We'll check in regularly and see how you're doing," was all that Mom would give me.

Patrick stopped the rental car, but I didn't open my door. I wasn't going to make them drag me in, but I was damn sure not gonna make this easy for them. Patrick popped the trunk and grabbed my suitcase, and Mom opened the door. A wave of Mid-western heat and humidity fell on me like a wet blanket. I saw Mom's mouth moving, but I had Slayer going too loud to hear what she was saying.

Then Mom did something pretty unlike her: She reached down and yanked my iPod cord, ripping the earbuds out of my tender ears.

"Ah, God, Mom, what the hell!" I yelled.

"You listen to me," she said. "I know you're not happy about this. I'm not happy about this either. But that does not mean you're going to be awful to me. I'm trying"— and there were tears in her eyes, which made me feel bad, but I wasn't giving in that easy—"I'm trying to get you some help. It's hard for both of us, but I need you to be safe and I don't know how to do that at this point. And as hard as it is for me to live with sending you here, it would be impossible to live with you actually succeeding in kill-ing yourself. That's what being a mom is about, Justin. You do anything to protect your kids. This is the only thing I know how to do right now."

And she was still crying, and I felt like a toad, or anyway something really low and disgusting. I was still pissed, but I got out of the car and decided to walk willingly through the heavy wooden front doors.

The words *Miss Doherty's Home for Wayward Girls* were engraved in the stone at the entrance. I was at the point of turning to Mom and making a joke—"Wayward girls? Hot!"—before I walked inside, but then I remembered I was mad at her and this joke probably wouldn't help my case that I didn't have sexual issues, so I didn't say anything.

A middle-aged, slightly chubby woman came out of the office to greet us. "Welcome," she said.

"Are you Miss Doherty?" I asked.

She gave me a smile in return. Not even the annoyance I was hoping for. "You must be Justin," she said. "Come on in, and we'll go over the rules and the treatment program."

She walked us through another wooden door into the office, which was nowhere near as old and gothic and creepy as the outside of the building. The walls were a soothing pale yellow, with colorful landscapes and pictures of flowers.

She steered us to a comfy couch where we awkwardly moved around, trying to figure out who should sit next to whom. We ended up with Mom in the middle, flanked by me and Patrick. Mom held Patrick's hand with her left and reached out for mine with her right, but she didn't get it.

Seated across from us in one lushly upholstered chair and three plastic classroom chairs were "Miss Doherty," who hadn't introduced herself, a young guy with a Moses beard and a Band of Horses T-shirt, an old guy with an awesome gray mustache, and a young woman who might be pretty if she had better clothes and hair and makeup.

"So," Miss Doherty said, "I am Helen Campbell, executive director of Heartland Academy. This," she said, gesturing at the old guy, "is Jack, who runs the SR group"—I didn't know what that was—"Tina,"—the plain young woman—"who runs Anger Management, and Max,"—Band of Horses Guy— "who'll be Justin's primary therapist and treatment director."

"What's up?" he said, extending a hand to me.

"I get it. You're the young, cool one who I can really open up to because you dig the kids of today. Am I right?"

He wouldn't take the bait and get mad. What the hell was it with these people anyway?

He kept his hand extended. "You know, it's rude to leave somebody hanging when they want to shake your hand," he said.

"You don't say," I said, keeping my arms folded across my chest.

Mom elbowed me in the ribs and hissed, "Justin!" under her breath.

"It's okay, Mom," Helen Campbell said. "This is a stressful time, and we're pretty used to new students acting out. I'm sure you've been over the handbook by now"—Mom went over it, but I'd tuned out when she was talking and definitely didn't look at it on my own—"so let me just go over the highlights."

The "highlights" of the rules took, no shit, forty-five minutes to go through. There was a six-level system here. I would be starting at level one. When I got to six I'd get to go home. Not because

I'd be fixed, but because I'd have achieved, apparently, "balance and wholeness."

No going into anybody else's room. Ever. No sexual contact with anybody. They didn't mention whether that included yourself, but they had staff members randomly strolling into your room whenever they felt like. Unclear what happened if you were tugging one out at the time. I didn't ask.

Real classes from 8:00-1:00, therapy bullshit all afternoon, then supervised study hall, "recreation time," which included no Internet and no TV, since pretty much anything on TV or in a movie was a trigger for somebody.

So, to sum up: No fun, creepy hippies watching my every move, and I had to talk about shit I'd rather not talk about pretty much every day.

In other words, I was in hell.

Finally the intake meeting ended, Mom and Patrick left, and a colossal guy who introduced himself as Tiny and didn't say another word walked me to my dorm room at Heartland Academy. And no, I did not give my mom a hug good-bye, because the hell with her.

First, Tiny rifled through my luggage, during which a 16G USB drive full of top-shelf porn was confiscated, and then there was a strip search, which involved a finger where no finger should be, at least not one attached to a gigantic linebacker-looking guy named Tiny. Finally, he took my laptop away for "virus removal," which I guess meant "de-pornification." I'd be allowed to use it for class-related word processing and PowerPoint purposes and nothing else. So no games, no Internet, nothing. It was basically going to be a fancy typewriter.

When we got to my room on the third floor, my roommate was sitting next to the gigantic window, which was helpfully covered in suicide-prevention bars. He didn't introduce himself. He was black, and very dark-skinned, and to judge by the people we saw in the airport and on the drive here, the only black person in, like, a hundred mile radius.

"I'm Justin," I said. He didn't acknowledge me. "So what are you in for?" I asked.

"What? What do you mean?"

"I mean, why are you at Heartland Academy? Did you try to off yourself? Drug problem? OCD?"

"None of your fucking business why I'm here," he said.

"I tried to kill myself. Tylenol. And my dad walked in on what should have been a wonderful blow job. From a chick. I should point that out. And I failed all my classes last year and I'm pretty much an asshole."

My roommate didn't say anything. "And I guess I'm not the only one," I said.

It was only four thirty. All I wanted to do was sleep, but I couldn't seem to manage that, so I just hung out on my bed and stared up at the ceiling until they called us for dinner.

3.

EMMY

"SO WHAT CLASSES ARE YOU TAKING THIS QUARTER?" THE LADY in the green sweatshirt with *Staff* embroidered on it asked as she ran her hands down my sides, around my legs, over my back.

The question barely registered. To try and get my mind off the awkward situation, I was busy wondering whether *Staff* was her last name or the position she held at this godforsaken place; how I was going to get my parents to bust me out of here for Simon's Rock by September; and what in hell I was going to do to distract myself from the growling hunger pains in my stomach. At home, I would've just worked out on our basement exercise equipment or drank a million Diet Cokes or both.

Here, it seemed neither was going to be available to me.

"Huh?"

"Classes start tomorrow, and they usually offer fun electives during the second summer term. So I was wondering what you were taking," she said, handing me my regular clothes. "I'll wait right outside the door. Let me know when you're dressed."

As soon as she left, I balled up the hospital gown and chucked it in the corner, then grabbed my jeans and pulled them on. They slid over my thighs and butt really easily, making me smile for the first time all day. I'd just bought them a few weeks back, to celebrate the momentous occasion of *finally* fitting into a size zero. Somehow, though, hitting the big milestone hadn't been nearly as satisfying as I'd imagined, so now I had my sights set on a chic double zero.

"Ready!" I called once I'd buttoned my jeans and pulled a plain black T-shirt over my head.

Ms. Staff came back and started digging through my duffel bag like we were at the airport and she'd seen something sketchy on the X-ray machine at security. She put most of my outfits—but not all—into one pile, while personal grooming items like razors, scissors, and tweezers went in another. I assumed this was to make it easier for me to put my stuff away in the appropriate places when she was done. Wherever that might be. "So, classes?" she asked again.

I stuck my hand into the front pocket of my jeans and

rummaged around for the schedule the head of school had given me in orientation. My hip bone poked into my palm as I pulled out the small, folded-up piece of paper, giving me a cheap little thrill. Not because it felt good—it didn't, the bone was actually sharp enough to really hurt—but because it meant I must be getting closer to my goal. I figured if I could just lose a little more weight, I'd stop hating my body so much—like my thighs, which rubbed together repulsively when I walked, or my belly, which folded over the top of my underwear in a heinous roll when I sat down.

"Uh, let's see. I have The Contemporary American Family . . . Women and the Media . . . and Body Politics," I said, reading the names of my classes off. "Oh, and yoga. Nope, nothing fun. Some girl next to me had *CSI* Science on her schedule. I totally could've gone for that one."

"They generally put students in the classes that will help them the most," the lady said, still feeling around inside my bag like she expected to discover hidden Baggies of pot, a bottle of Jack, and maybe a vibrator in there. I hated to disappoint, but she wasn't going to find a thing: Pot led to the munchies, so for obvious reasons it was out; ditto for alcohol, which was full of empty calories; and I'd been doing just fine in the guy department, so no need for any autoerotica. Or at least I *thought* I'd been doing fine in the guy department, until a few months ago. "So can you figure out why those particular classes were chosen for you?"

I contemplated my schedule again. I didn't think anything on it would be a help to anyone unless they were planning on becoming a total feminazi. And I wasn't. "Not so much," I said, then added, "So the girl with the purple hair who gets to go on field trips to the morgue . . . are they trying to stop her from becoming a serial killer? Or is she already one?"

Staffie just laughed, leaving me to worry that maybe I'd been right.

"Come on, you can tell me," I said. "Seriously, I need to know if I should avoid her in the caf or whatever."

She provided me exactly zero answers and one pile of clothes. "You can put these in your dresser now."

I stared at the smaller pile she hadn't handed me. It consisted of tank tops and belly shirts and short-shorts, all of which I could finally wear without feeling too horribly self-conscious. "What about those?"

"They're against the dress code," she said with an apologetic smile. "We'll put them in storage and your mom and dad can bring them home after Family Weekend, along with these." She pointed to my personal grooming items.

"But how am I going to shave . . . or tweeze my eyebrows . . . or cut my nails?" I asked. This place was getting more insane by the second.

"You can use a home-waxing kit instead of shaving, and go to the nurse when you want to trim your nails. She keeps clippers in her office," she told me. "Honestly, you're here to get better, not find a date to the prom. You'll be working so hard on yourself, you won't care that your legs are a little hairy."

"That is so . . . so . . . demeaning!" I sputtered. "What good could it possibly do to treat us like such babies?"

"Think of it this way," she said, putting a gentle but firm hand on my shoulder and steering me toward my dresser. "Babies need help learning how to navigate the world without hurting themselves or others. The same holds true for our students."

After she left, I put away the clothes Heartland actually let me keep and plopped down on my bed. I had a horrible pit in my stomach. It had suddenly hit me that I wasn't just all alone in this unfamiliar room, I was all alone in the freaking *world*. My parents had given up on me just as sure as my real parents had given me up. I pressed my fingers against my temples, willing the tears to go away at least until lights-out—which was still five-plus hours away—when I could cry without anyone seeing.

I'd almost succeeded in stemming the tide when a kid my age I assumed was Farm Girl walked in the room. "Hi," I said, swiping quickly at my face to make sure there was no sign of weakness there. "I'm Emmy. And you must be—"

The girl gave me a little wave but didn't say a word.

"You must be . . ." I tried again. Still nothing. I prayed I didn't utter the words Farm Girl just to fill the awkward silence. Eventually, I gave up on waiting and finished the sentence for her. ". . . my roommate."

She nodded. Then she sat down on her bed, grabbed a journal and a pen from her desk, and started scribbling away.

"Great to meet you," I said, though so far, not so much.

My roommate looked up for a nanosecond, smiled slightly, and went back to writing.

I gave it one last shot. "How long have you been here?"

She gave me a noncommittal shrug.

Seeing as I had no one to talk to and no idea what to do with myself until dinner, I grabbed the the only book currently on my bookshelf. It was Sean Covey's *The 7 Habits of Highly Effective Teens*. I guessed *Thirteen Reasons Why* had been confiscated along with my tank tops and tweezers. "This yours?" I asked my roommate.

She shook her head, then wrote something on a scrap of paper, and held it out to me. Farm Girl obviously wasn't deaf, but apparently she was mute. I grabbed the note from her hand. *Required reading for all students*, it said.

"Okay, gotcha. Thanks."

I figured I might as well get it out of the way sooner rather than later, so I flipped the book open to a random spot. It talked about how sticking to your principles is the key to success and ignoring them means you'll fail. No new news there. I read on. Next the author talked about how principles apply to everyone, everywhere, and cannot be viewed as belonging to a single gender, class or religion, or nation–and the specific example used was principles are not "American or Chinese."

It wigged me out. Why did the one page I'd landed on mention being Chinese? It was like the book knew me and had specifically picked where I should start. I decided it must be haunted like the rest of the place.

That was the only semi-interesting thing Joss and I had uncovered about Heartland in all our Google-powered research: It used to be a home for "wayward girls." Today, those same girls would probably get cast on *16 and Pregnant* and put on the cover of *People* magazine, but back in the day they got sent away for being an embarrassment to their families. Supposedly, there were tons of ghost babies wailing piteously for their mommies, and girls crying just as hard for their never-to-be-seen-or-heard-from-again kids roaming the halls of this place at night.

At home, with Joss, all this had seemed kind of funny. Now it was just plain creepy.

And things only went from bad to worse when a student mentor—a girl named Alisha on level five, which meant she was *this close* to getting sprung from Heartland—came to escort me to the cafeteria for dinner.

"Okay, so it's my job to tell you the rules. And the rules are, you have to have a protein, a grain, a fruit, and a vegetable at every meal," she told me as she plunked an *obscene* amount of food on our plates. "And you have to finish your entire meal, too."

I stared at her like she was from another planet. To me, she actually was: The Planet F-A-T. I felt sorry for her. If I still felt this bad after losing twenty pounds, she must absolutely *despise* herself.

"Sorry," she said, shaking her head like *Hey, what can you do?* "They're really strict with us eating-disordered girls."

A familiar anger radiated through my body, starting at my toes and working its way up until even my hair felt mad. Really? That was what my parents had told Heartland to get me locked up here? Wow. What a crime. All I'd done was get rid of some stubborn baby chub. I didn't have a problem. *They* were the ones who had a problem—with me.

"You . . . " I started, but the words got stuck in my throat. I cleared it and tried again. "Have an eating disorder? Had, I mean?"

The girl patted her bulging belly. If I didn't know better, I would've thought she was a wayward ghost girl who haunted the halls at night. "You'll find out pretty soon you can't actually get *rid* of an eating disorder. You spend the rest of your life *recovering* from one."

If that was what recovery looked like, I'd rather die, not that I told Alisha that. "Sorry, that must be hard," I said. "But I actually don't have an eating disorder. I'm here because I got kicked out of school for bullying some douche bag on Facebook. Unofficially, though, I kinda think my parents were just sick of people asking them who the little Chinese chick was."

31

Alisha looked at me with something like pity in her eyes. Which is exactly how I looked back at her and her muffin top. "Save it for your therapist," she said. "For now, you have to put the required amount of calories on your plate and eat them all."

There was no freaking way I'd worked this hard to look half decent only to have it taken away from me by some blubber-loving freaks. Although I only resorted to purging on days I accidentally ate a little too much air-popped popcorn or grabbed a second fat-free, sugar-free yogurt, it was becoming clear I'd have to rely on this tactic a little more heavily here.

Like, after every single meal.

It wasn't ideal, but nothing about this situation was. Whatever it took to keep from ballooning up like an Oompa Loompa again was what I was willing to do. A little pain so I wouldn't gain. Totally worth it.

Pudgemeister Alisha and I carried our two-ton trays to a table and sat down. I nibbled at the corn kernels drowning in buttery sauce, feeling entirely nauseous and wondering how I was going to wait to go to the bathroom to puke and not do it right here, right now.

This guy across from me was watching as I pushed the yellow mush around on my plate. "You anorexic or something? Is that why you're in this lovely therapeutic setting?"

I wanted to tell him to shut up and mind his own business, but he was kind of cute. Okay, totally my type. He had that skinny, lost-puppy-dog, indie-rocker kind of thing going. If I hadn't sworn off of guys forever, I might've given this one a second look.

"Nah, bullying," I started to explain, but Alisha chimed in before I could finish.

"Justin, you may not ask other new students about their issues at mealtime. We talk about those sorts of things during groups, which start tomorrow along with regular classes. The therapists can maintain appropriate boundaries there. For now, try to stick to less controversial topics."

"Oh sorry," he said, giving me a wink. "Let me rephrase my question: Does your bullying of the corn have anything to do with why you're here?"

I tried to play hard to get by looking pissed but ended up laughing instead. "Only according to my parents, who needed an excuse to get rid of me. You?"

He gave me a sly little smile, and it made his eyes kind of look like someone had thrown glitter in them. They reminded me of the sparkly green lava lamp Joss had given me for my eleventh birthday. I'd wanted to bring it to Heartland—I got kind of nervous in the dark, as embarrassing as that might be for a sixteen-year-old to admit—but personal furnishings weren't allowed. Along with cute clothes and hair removal devices and cell phones and the Internet and everything else fun in this world.

"Same kind of deal," he said with a shrug. "Hey, can I just say you're the first semi-cool person I've met since I got here? The rest are, like, totally nuts."

His sort-of compliment made me miss my clothes and personal grooming items even more. How I was supposed to have a chance at a normal relationship here wearing shapeless sweats and sporting furry legs, a unibrow, and ape pits? I mean, yeah, I knew relationships weren't allowed, and that I wasn't even allowing myself any more of them until college, but it would've been nice to at least dream without the specter of unwanted fuzz hanging over my fantasies.

Alisha chimed in again. "You need to refrain from name-calling, Justin. This is a nonjudgmental environment."

We both ignored her. "Tell me about it. My roomie"—I aimed a thumb at Jenny, which was what Alisha had told me Farm Girl's real name was on the way to the caf, and who was sitting way at the end of the table—"won't say a word. Just gives me basic sign language and writes me a note once in a while. Alisha here finally explained she has a form of this thing called selective mutism, so she won't speak in groups or to new people even though she does with her family and friends, and I guess her therapist here. I feel bad for her and all, but I'm gonna go crazy without anyone to talk to."

Justin gave me more of the green-eyed glitter treatment. "You'll have me to talk to."

"Good to know," I said, feeling an odd little flirty flutter in my stomach. Or maybe it was just more nausea from having to eat so much. Hard to tell.

"And if it makes you feel any better, my roommate won't talk to me either, and he doesn't even have anything to blame it it on. Honestly, he's just an asshole."

I burst out laughing, and the combo platter of what Justin had just said and my response to it pushed Alisha over the edge.

"You—" she said, pointing at Justin. "I said no name-calling. And as for you"—she pointed at me here—"you better watch yourself. Any more crap and I'll get you put in the SR group with the hard-core dykes. They'll love your skinny little ass."

"What's SR?" Justin asked, pulling a crumpled piece of paper from his pocket. "I'm assigned to a *SR* group and I'm just wondering if the hard-core dykes are going to appreciate my manly hetero presence in there."

Another one of the green sweatshirted staff walked by and Alisha fell right back into therapy robot mode. "*SR* stands for 'Sexual Reactivity' and no, you won't be placed in the gay girl's group." Once the Staffer was out of hearing range, she glared back at me. "You, I'm not so sure about."

I pulled my schedule out of my pocket, and there were those awesome hip bones jutting into my palms again. They made me even more determined not to eat, or at least not hold down, the steaming globs of goo Alisha was trying to force-feed me. "Nope, I won't be there either. Apparently, I'll be in a thrilling

Adoption Issues group instead, after which I have . . . " I scanned the paper and then snapped. ". . . a freaking Anger Management one? Crap! Why does everyone think I'm so angry?"

I guess I was yelling a little bit, because the whole table turned to stare at me. Even Jenny, who tended not to acknowledge stuff going on around her, gaped at me wide-eyed.

"Yeah, it's probably because you start screaming every time something doesn't go your way," Alisha said with a smirk.

"I don't scream every time I don't get my way!" I practically screamed at her. I know, the irony. But I was *pissed*.

Alisha just laughed. "I can see that."

Justin put his hand on top of mine. The weight and warmth of it felt nice, like snuggling under a heavy blanket on a rainy day. Right before Alisha yelled at him for "touching me inappropriately," he said, "Don't worry. I'll be there with you, too. We'll have fun yelling at everyone else."

Alisha gave me the stink eye until I finished all the food on my plate. I was so full and disgusted with myself by the time I finally did, I could barely wait to get to the bathroom. "Be back in a sec," I said, trying to look ultracasual and not as sweaty, sick, and desperate as I was feeling. "Just have to brush my teeth before study hall starts."

Alisha gave me a knowing look. "I have to 'brush my teeth,' too," she said, using her fingers to make air quotes. "I'll go with you."

"Yell with you tomorrow," Justin said. "Try not to get into too much trouble before then."

"You, too," I called over my shoulder.

I walked down the hall super-fast, trying to burn some of the calories I wasn't going to be able to get rid of—it wasn't realistic to think *everything* would come up—but no matter how much speed I put on, Alisha was right there beside me.

"Forgot to tell you another rule they have for ED kids here," she said, panting. Clearly all that chowing down had not only wreaked havoc on her figure, it had also made her grossly out of shape. "Your feet have to face the right way in the bathroom, if you get my drift."

"I have no idea what you're talking about," I told her, slamming through the girls' room door and into a stall, although of course I did. She'd pretty much read my mind.

I sat down on the toilet without even pulling down my pants and rested my head in my hands. Once again, tears were threatening to spill and if I started crying now, I was afraid I'd never stop. I hoped my parents were happy—so far, this place had been *amazing* for my mood and self-esteem. Not. I was madder and more depressed than ever, with the exception of a few minutes at dinner when I'd talked to a semi-cute guy who'd thought I was semi-cool.

Alisha interrupted my pity party by rapping on the door. The sharp, tinny sound echoed around the tiled bathroom, making my head hurt along with my stomach. "You done yet?"

"Almost," I said, giving her the finger from behind the door. I'd considered using the container on the wall meant for used tampons and pads as my puke bucket, but then I opened it and found it completely full. It never would have held the entire contents of my stomach, and besides—*ewwwww*. I did not want to get hit in the face with someone else's former uterine wall. I was just going to have to ride this one out until I could ditch Alisha. The timing was definitely not ideal—the longer I waited, the more of what I'd eaten would get digested, the more calories I'd have consumed, the faster I'd get fat again—but I didn't have much of a choice.

I flushed the toilet, walked out of the stall, and washed my hands. "I'm going to evening study hall now. See you later, Alisha." I was hoping she'd leave so I could just get on with it.

But she gave me another *I can see right through you* look. "I'm going, too, so I'll walk you there."

"Great," I muttered.

"I guess you forgot your toothbrush?" she asked, smirking again.

I shrugged. This place truly sucked.

CHAPTER 4

JUSTIN

SECOND SUMMER TERM HERE WAS APPARENTLY LIGHT ON THE academics. I had Aesthetics of Classic Film, which should at least help me catch up on my sleep; Culinary Science, which should be kind of interesting since I wasn't allowed to have any sharp objects; Fitness, which ought to be exciting, since the so-called normal kids at my regular high school got kind of *Lord of the Flies* in the boys' locker room, so who knew what the population here would be like; and Art Appreciation.

And then there were my therapy sessions. And Sexual Reactivity group. And Anger Management group. Because, in addition to having suicidal ideation and sexual reactivity, I apparently had anger "issues." I hated that word. Issues. It reminded me of comic books. In our next issue, can Justin stop himself from calling his mom a heartless bitch? (Nope!) In our next issue, does Justin finally grow a pair and tell his dad he's a selfish asshole? (Yep!) Is this, more than blowjobus interruptus, the real reason Justin got shipped off to Heartland? (Quite possibly. Dad didn't much care for hearing the truth.)

Tiny dropped me off at the therapy room, where Max, aka Moses, was sitting in a leather chair. He gestured at a beanbag chair and a couch, and said, "Wherever you want, Justin."

"About two thousand miles from here is where I want," I said.

He didn't laugh or respond. He just tapped on an iPad.

"So you get iPads?"

"The whole treatment team has them," he answered.

"Awesome. How much porn does it hold?"

"Let's talk about why you're here, shall we?" he said.

"Don't you have it in my file? Right on your screen there?"

"I have what the intake form says. What do you say?"

"I pulled a prank that went too far."

"What was that?"

I rolled my eyes. "It was my so-called suicide attempt, when I swallowed too many Tylenols. I mean, we have Percocets in the house from when Mom got her hand surgery, you know? I could have downed a bunch of those and gone nighty-night permanently. So it clearly wasn't a serious attempt. It was just, like, a prank."

"Hilarious prank," Max said, tapping on the iPad. Jerk.

"You know what I mean. I was just—I needed some attention, that's all."

Max looked up from the screen. "Why?"

I knew why, of course. But I wasn't feeling that way right now. And I was afraid if I started talking about it, that would make it all real again. And then I didn't know what was going to happen. So I just answered, "I don't know."

Max smiled at me. "Well, when you're ready to be honest about that, we'll know you're making some progress." God, I hated this guy. I really would like to sneak up on him in the middle of the night and shave his stupid Moses beard off.

After fifty minutes, Tiny walked me and several other guys to SR group. SR group was all *guys*, what the hell, and seemed to be an excuse for everybody in the group to brag about all the action they'd gotten and how it left them feeling sad and empty inside. I didn't say anything, because apart from the blow job that wasn't, there was only the hand job last year and a couple of boob gropes. Oh, and one totally awkward and, okay, not very skilled journey into Kat Masterson's panties, which may or may not have had anything to do with her dumping me the next day.

That was it for me. Whereas everybody else in this group, it seemed, had been busy putting their dicks pretty much anywhere they could. After the group ended, I went up to the gray-haired, awesome-mustached guy named Jack who ran the group. "Uh, Mr. Inghoff?" I began. I had no idea what his real last name was, but my stupid masturbation joke seemed pretty appropriate in this group. "Jack? I think I'm in the wrong group here."

He looked at me through his John Lennon glasses, and I was so distracted by a tiny blob of spit trapped in his mustache that I almost didn't hear him say, "Yeah, Justin, everybody says that at first. Everybody *else* has issues. *I* don't belong here. These people are *crazy*." Old Jack had a kind of crazy glint in his eye as he said this, which made me think he was a little crazy himself. "And you just made a sophomoric sex joke about my name, which doesn't really help your case."

Damn. Didn't think of that. "No, Jack. You don't understand. These guys get their rocks off more times before breakfast than I have in my entire life."

Jack looked for a second like he might crack a smile, but then his face got kind of stern. "Justin. We're not here to judge other people's issues."

"Well, why the hell would you put us in groups then? Jesus Christ, this is fucking retarded!"

Jack pulled out his iPad and gave the screen a few taps. "Okay, Justin. That's five demerit points. Since you're at level one, you can't go down any levels—"

"You said, 'go down,'" I said, since I was in the shit already. "Don't they tell you not to say stuff like that around the pervs?"

He kept talking like I hadn't said anything. "But if you want to be able to move up a level, to have any privileges at all, you need to work on getting ahold of yourself. I'm making a note of this incident."

I came back with a British accent, doing my best Minerva McGonagall, which, admittedly, was not very good. "*Ten points from Gryffindor!* You guys are the lamest people on the face of the earth. I honestly don't know what keeps you assholes from killing yourselves every night, because if I looked like you and had to say shit like that every day, I would have popped something a lot stronger than Tylenol."

Jack tapped on his iPad again, maybe a little more vigorously than last time. "You'd better run along," he said. "Don't want to be late for . . ." He checked his screen. ". . . looks like Anger Management." He flashed me a smile, a smile that said, "You little snot, I hear worse than that every day, and if you think you've gotten under my skin, you're dreaming." At least that's what I thought it said.

Another big dude who was not Tiny (or, tiny, for that matter) escorted me from SR to AM because apparently I might try to kill myself if they let me walk down the hall by myself. But it wasn't me I felt like killing.

The AM group was at least coed. Emmy, the anorexic Asian girl I'd met at dinner who seemed kind of normal—at least compared to my grumpy roommate and the pervs in SR—was there. There was a seat next to her, but I didn't take it. I was afraid if they saw me sitting by her, they'd make that a privilege they could take away from me. So I took it away from myself.

My roomie was there, too, as was Emmy's silent roomie Jenny. Then there was a little white girl who looked really young and another white boy who reminded me of the mullet-sporting guy who ran The Beast at King's Island when I was there on Memorial Day weekend.

We all sat silently and the therapist, the plain young woman from my intake meeting, came in and said, "Well, it's the beginning of a new term and we've got a couple of new members here today. Let's make them feel comfortable by introducing ourselves."

My roommate, Mohammed, actually revealed that he got sent here as an alternative sentence after his second assault with a dangerous weapon, which I'll admit was going to make me a little more cautious about trying to bait him into speech back in the room.

Tina, the facilitator, looked at him for a long time after he said that. "Anything else you'd like to add?" she asked.

"Nope," he said.

The mullet kid was named Chip. He was from Ohio, which raised the odds that he actually was the kid who ran The Beast.

Emmy's silent roomie didn't talk, of course, and the little girl, the one who looked really young, refused to introduce herself. "This," the therapist said, "is Jenny, who has a form of selective mutism and is working on speaking to others within social situations such as this one, but is not quite ready to do so yet. And next to her is Diana."

"She lets her fists do the talking," Chip said, laughing, and Diana looked up for the first time and gave Chip a look that drained all the laughter out of him.

Tina ignored the brewing fight. "Now, I'll have our new members introduce themselves and, if you two feel comfortable sharing this, talk a little bit about why you think you're here?"

There was an awkward silence, and I looked over at Emmy, who stared back at me. *You first*, she mouthed. Okay.

"I'm Justin. I was just thinking about how one little space is all that separates *therapist* from 'the rapist.'" I paused for the laugh. Nobody laughed except Emmy. Tough crowd. I smiled at the one appreciative audience member. "Seems like this is the group I actually belong in, not that Sexual Reactivity group, which they put me in because my dad walked in on me getting blown. I'll be the first to admit that *that* little scene is going to need some working out in a therapeutic setting, but I hardly think it means I should be in the man-whore group."

Only my roommate cracked a smile at my use of "man whore."

"Justin, I appreciate you've acknowledged that you should be here, even if you broke about three other rules in that speech."

"Are you gonna tap on your little screen like Jack and give me the ten points from Gryffindor treatment?"

The rapist smiled. "Do you think Gryffindor is where you

belong? I mean, it's the one most people choose because all the main characters are there, but really, is that where you'd sort yourself if this were Hogwarts?"

"If this were Hogwarts, I'd sort myself right next to Emma Watson," I said, which maybe wasn't going to help my case that I didn't belong in the SR group, so I followed with, "Gryffindor is the courageous one, right? I mean, I'm here because I have the balls to tell adults when they're being douche bags, so yeah, Gryffindor."

5.

EMMY

AFTER MY FAILED POST-DINNER PURGING ATTEMPT, THERE WAS the failed attempt after study hall, the one during reflective time, and the one right before bed. If it wasn't Alisha following me around and getting in the way of my plans, it was one of the green-sweatshirted Staffies. Anger Management group was actually going to be the perfect place for me if I didn't figure out a way around the annoying over-supervision of my bodily functions soon.

And that wasn't my only frustration. There was also not being able to fall asleep at the strictly enforced ten thirty lights-out time, especially in our pitch-black, silent room. I'd nervously tossed and turned most of the night, the contents in my belly sloshing around loudly as I hoped and wished for a miracle. As in, I *hoped* my restlessness was at least burning off a fraction of what I'd consumed at dinner, and I *wished* the damn window would open so I could hurl out of it, then hurl *myself* out of it and escape.

Toss, turn. Turn, toss.

I kept waiting for the ghost baby and baby mama wails to start up, but all I heard were the night staff's footsteps as they patrolled the hall and, occasionally, our door opening. That always happened right as I was starting to relax. The noise and intrusion made my heart jump and then race, and the flashlight shining around the room got me wired in the worst possible way. I wondered if I'd ever be able to sleep again, or at least as long I was here at Heartland. Chances seemed pretty slim.

I guess I must have eventually passed out, though, because the next thing I knew, the PA system was blaring the morning announcements. I forced my eyes open and saw Farm Girl holding a sign in front of my face.

Rise and shine. It's time for yoga.

"I hate yoga," I mumbled, pulling a pillow over my head.

She grabbed it and threw it across the room.

"Fine," I said, rolling out of bed and grabbing some yoga pants and a T-shirt from my drawer. I tucked myself between the wall and dresser to put them on, as far out of my roomie's view as possible.

Yoga turned out to be meditation and some verrrry light

stretching with shavasana—the part where you just lie there like roadkill—thrown in at the end. The instructor chanted a bunch of hoo-ha about loving our bodies and being grateful for their strength, but all I could think was *You got me up for this? Dead people could work out harder.*

Breakfast was another anxiety-inducing feast—scrambled eggs, toast, tomatoes, and slimy canned peaches—that I once again couldn't dispose of, either before I choked it down or afterward, due to the nosy, ever-present staff. By that point— and it was only eight thirty in the morning—I was so crabby and groggy from too little sleep and too much food I would have loved to spend the rest of the day hiding out under the covers, but instead I had to go to my academic courses. Making a kid go to school in July is just plain criminal. There should seriously be a law against it.

Still, I dragged my ass from class to class, pinching myself throughout the periods just to stay awake. Jury was still out on the subject matter. First days were always the boring-awkward combo platter of talking about what we were *going to* talk about all semester plus the embarrassing get-to-know-each-other games, so I was reserving judgment.

On to lunch. The plateful of greasy tacos, broccoli, beans, and banana was a total gastric nightmare. My stomach felt like a bloated beach ball and there seemed to be a permanent lump in my throat, which was where I figured all the food I'd been forced to shove down my gullet in the past twenty-four hours stopped.

Afternoon at School for Screwups was dedicated to head-shrinking, so then I got herded off to Adoption Issues group. I would have given my left ovary for a Red Bull Total Zero. Instead, I got a lukewarm bottle of water and learned that I Wasn't Alone and My Feelings Were Very Normal.

Finally, it was time for Anger Management. In a weird way, I was almost kind of looking forward to it. First, because it meant I'd survived my first full day of classes and therapy bullshit without going totally insane and second, because I'd get to see Justin, the cute guy I'd met in the caf last night. I figured I'd have to dazzle him with my sparkling personality and half-decent bod now, before I pudged out again and he was too disgusted to look at me like that.

I was already camped out on the sagging tan velour sofa when he walked in. I gave him a big smile, hoping for a glittery green-eyed one back. Instead, he blew me off and went and sat on the love seat next to a dude with a mullet. Bummer. More awkward introductions, then a Hogwarts sorting game no one wanted to participate in.

"Come on now, people. Justin said he'd be sorted in Gryffindor because he has courage. How about the rest of you?" Tina, the therapist running the Anger Management group, asked.

Not sure what she was trying to accomplish, because the

odds were Chip the Mullethead was illiterate; Jenny my mute roommate was never going to answer; and Diana (and probably Mohammed, based on his explanation why he ended up in this group) would prefer to beat the shit out of J. K. Rowling than read her books. But I decided to play along anyhow because for one thing, I love Harry Potter and another, I wanted to see how Justin might react when he heard my affiliation.

"Ravenclaw," I announced, sneaking a look at him to see if he'd give me a thumbs-up or furrow his brow or what. "And not just because that's where the Asian girl is. But because they're the brainiacs, the quirky smart kids who are valued for their individuality instead of made fun of for it."

Justin gave me a little upward tilt of the chin when I was done with my confession, so I figured we were cool despite our different HP houses. Everyone else acted like they hadn't even heard me.

Seeing as she was getting absolutely nowhere with her attempts to get us to bond in Pottermore, Tina moved on to another tactic. "Fine then. Let's go at this from a different angle. I want everyone to tell the group what your favorite breakfast is and why."

We all stared at her. No one said a word.

"I'll start," Tina said breezily, like it didn't bother her we wanted no part of her games. "I love bran flakes cereal because it gets my morning off to a good start."

"More like a good fart," Chip hooted. Then he let out a huge guffaw, cupped his hand under his armpit, and let a few fake ones rip.

"Grow up," I muttered. I couldn't believe my parents would pay for this kind of an education—fart jokes were so second grade—and not the college-level one I could have been getting at Simon's Rock.

"What? You pissed because your favorite thing for breakfast is your finger?" Chip said, squinting. I couldn't tell if he was making an Asian, sexual, or eating disorder joke.

I tried my best to ignore whichever he had been going for. "Could you be any more of an uneducated, immature, misogynistic pig?"

Jenny whipped her head around, gave me a death stare, and started scribbling in her journal. Then she ripped out a piece of paper and stomped over to give it to me. *Take it back!* it read.

"Why?" I asked "Face it, that's what he is. A total pig."

Jenny shook her head furiously. I guess she liked her men dumb and insulting.

"I like breast meat in the morning," Diana piped in with a demented cackle. "The whiter, the better."

"Nutritionists stress the importance of protein at each meal, Diana. Chicken is a great source, even if it is a tad unconventional for breakfast," Tina replied, unfazed by the disturbingly evil laugh coming from such a cute little person.

"Who said anything about chicken?" Diana asked, sticking

"Contrary to what Chip may think," I jumped in, hoping to move on without any more weird drama, "my favorite breakfast food is actually a bagel with cream cheese and bacon." I hadn't actually eaten a "bacon-bagel-burger," as I liked to call my creation, in over six months, but I sometimes dreamed of them. I'd wake up crying, thinking I'd actually eaten one, then cry some more because I knew I could never really eat one again if I wanted to stay thin.

I was still mourning the loss of the salty, creamy, carbo goodness when a balled-up piece of paper whipped me in the head. "What the hell?" I yelled.

Jenny was glaring at me, her face flushed crimson.

"Ix-nay on the acon-bay," Chip whispered out of the side of his mouth. "Don't you have any clue why she stopped talking?"

"No," I said, uncrumpling the paper to read it. It was a long list entitled *Pigs Rule*. "How could I? She doesn't talk to me, remember?"

"Jenny, please refrain from throwing things or I'll be forced to give you demerit points. And Emmy, if it's okay with Jenny, perhaps you could read from the note aloud," Tina said, looking over at Jenny for confirmation. Jenny nodded emphatically.

"Uhhh, sure," I said, scanning the paper. It was actually kind of interesting, if maybe a little unbelievable. "'One, pigs snuggle each other when sleeping, and dream as much as humans do. Pigs like to play, sunbathe, and explore. At farm sanctuaries, they are reported to love music, playing soccer, and getting massages.'"

"It's good to be a pig!" Chip crowed.

Jenny gave him a big smile before frowning again in my direction. Then she rolled her hand and wrist at me in that universal *keep going* sign.

"'Two, pigs communicate constantly and have twenty different vocalizations. Mama pigs sing to their babies when they are nursing.' Awwww, cute!" I looked over at Justin to see if maybe he thought *I* was cute, but he was staring out the window, totally not listening. I went through the rest of the list without any more of my clearly uncute commentary." Let me see, 'Pigs have the mental capacity of a human three-year-old, a great sense of direction, can run up to eleven miles an hour, and are clean, do not sweat, and eat slowly and in moderation.'"

Tina was nodding happily. "Great point you make there, Jenny."

"Exactly what point did she make?" Justin chimed in. If he'd been listening he'd know . . . wait, no, that wasn't true. Because I'd read the list and I still had no idea what her point was.

"Seriously," I agreed. "I have no clue either."

"Well, that we shouldn't use the word pig as an insult, of course. Just like no one should ever use the word gay to mean uncool," Tina explained.

I sighed, more loudly than I intended to.

"You don't buy into that crap, huh, Emmy?" Diana said, excited to be the one calling someone else out. Her tears were all gone, and the demonic grin was back.

"I guess I was just thinking most stereotypes have some truth to them. So if pigs don't eat a lot or sweat, then how did expressions like *pigging out* and *sweating like a pig* get started?" I asked. I honestly was wondering. "And seriously . . . how could anyone possibly know if pigs dream as much as humans do? Are all the pigs like *I had that nightmare about my teeth falling out again* and then their pig friends are like *LOL, Freud said that one is subliminally about masturbation?*"

Justin kind of gave a little chuckle, which only fueled my desire to keep going. Guys liked funny girls, right? "Also, can you imagine a pig lying on a massage table saying, *Can you work my lower back some more? I must have pulled a muscle scoring that winning soccer goal yesterday.*"

Here Justin actually snorted. There was no stopping me now.

"So sorry, Jenny, that I didn't know discrimination against pigs was so rampant," I said, wrapping it up. "I'll try not to take their little piggy names in vain again."

Jenny, who looked like she was about to shoot lava out her ears, waved me over. Tina got all excited.

"I think she wants to tell you something," Tina said, clasping her hands together like she was thanking God for all her wonderful head-shrinking gifts.

I walked over to where Jenny was sitting. She hauled herself out of the beanbag, stood up, whispered "Fuck you" in my ear so quietly only I could hear it, and then socked me surprisingly hard in the gut.

And just like that—barf-o-rama. I couldn't have stopped the flood even if I'd wanted to. During the past six months of stealth purging, I'd had to learn to puke quickly and quietly by clenching my stomach. Only this time, Jenny had clenched it for me—with her fist.

I wouldn't have even felt bad about it—score one for me for getting rid of all those calories, and two for getting back at someone who'd just told me to f-off—except for the fact that Justin had witnessed it. Not sexy. No amount of laughs would make up for that kind of gross performance.

Though my lunch got tossed mostly on the floor, some of my regurgitated taco and from the looks of it, banana and broccoli, landed on Jenny's shoes. She took one look at her defiled blue canvas Toms and tackled me to the ground. At first, I tried to block her kicks and punches without really fighting back, but then gave up the whole pacifist thing and started scuffling hard.

"Pig pile!" I screamed, just because I knew it would piss off Jenny even more. Also I hoped it might be amusing enough to take Justin's mind off the fact that I'd just vomited extremely uncutely in front of him.

Diana must have felt left out because a few seconds later she came at us full force. "Pigs are delicious!" she whooped, diving in between Jenny and me. "And vegetarians are all ugly pussies with hairy armpits who won't wear makeup because it's tested on animals!"

Somewhere along the way, Chip and Justin had start beating the crap out of each other, too. Only Mohammed, whom I'd pegged as the biggest brawler of them all, stayed out of the fray.

Tina's calm request for us to stop fighting went ignored. Then she yelled at us to "Cut it out!" Still nothing. She tried pulling us off of each other. It was a total losing battle.

"Jenny stopped talking because the piglet she raised from birth won the 4-H fair, you asshole!" Chip screamed at me, even though he was using Justin as his punching bag. "Don't make fun of her and don't say the goddamn word *bacon*!"

"She's mute because her pig won? That's crazy!" I screamed back.

"No, because then they sell the winning pig. And slaughter it," Chip spat. "Her stepfather thought it was funny to tell her the next day the bacon she was eating was actually from her pig. She freaked out, stopped talking, and the rest is Heartland history."

"I'm sorry, Jenny. That's awful. I wish you'd told me before . . . or, I guess I mean, wrote me one of your notes about that before." I let go of her ponytail and dragged myself out of the catfight. Diana quit throwing jabs. Even Justin and Chip untangled themselves from each other and went back to their seats.

"Wilbur was the coolest pig ever," Jenny whispered, shaking and crying.

Tina started applauding. "Great group! We're really getting somewhere now."

She had to be kidding. I'd expected a million demerit points, demands for apologies, and kids getting a level drop—if they had any levels to go down to, which I didn't—but apparently not.

"I love the way you all communicated, despite the fight. Those are the first words Jenny has said in group since she came to Heartland eight months ago," Tina said, smiling. "So here's your assignment to keep this kind of great progress going: You are all responsible for each other's actions for the rest of the week. For our two new members, that means for the time being, your mentors and chaperones will now be the people in this room."

"Yes!" I whispered under my breath. That would get Alisha off my back, thankthefreakinglord.

Tina beamed at me. "Glad you're so excited about it, Emmy. As a group, you will make sure everyone does their chores, their homework, gets the proper nutrition, and makes it to class on time. If you succeed, you may all have your iPod for one hour this weekend and get an extra ten minutes in the required weekly call to your parents or guardians."

"And if we don't?" Justin asked.

"You'll keep on working as a team until you get it right," Tina told him.

CHAPTER 6

JUSTIN

BACK IN THE ROOM, I WAS EXAMINING MY BRUISES IN THE mirror, and Mohammed was smiling. "I liked the man-whore line," he said.

"Yeah. Thanks for having my back with the Chipster there," I said sarcastically as I looked at my arm where the Chipster's watch, or possibly fingernail, had left a long, slightly bloody scrape.

"Listen. You get yourself into something stupid, you get yourself out. I'm not here to clean up your mess. And I'm not going down a level for anybody. This place is like prison, you know? Do your own time."

I plopped down on my bed and found that my ass really hurt. No idea how that happened. "Well, according to Tina, we're all supposed to support each other and hold each other accountable so we can earn ten more minutes talking to our parents. Which, I mean, wow. Big deal."

Just like that, Mohammed was up off his bed and standing over me. "It is a big deal. And if you're the one who screws it up, I'm gonna hurt you in ways you can't even imagine."

Normally I'd back down from something like this, but having just mixed it up with Chip, I was feeling all full of testosterone. "What the hell is your problem?" I said, standing up. "You think I'm scared of you 'cause you're black or something? You've been a total dick ever since I got here, and just when I think we're having a normal conversation, you go all gangsta on me! What the hell's your issue?"

Mohammed stared at me for a minute with murder in his eyes. Then he started to smile and laugh. "That was racist in about five different ways," he said, and sat down on his bed. The crisis had apparently passed, but I wasn't sure why. Heartland Academy was like the inverse of the real world. Here, you said something racist to a black guy and it *stopped* a fight.

"Do you know anything about Sierra Leone?" he asked.

"Is that in Africa?"

Mohammed smiled. "Yes. It's in Africa."

"Okay, well, I guess I know a little more about it now, then," I said, smiling back a little though I didn't know exactly where we were going here.

"My mother and I escaped the civil war there. I watched my father die screaming."

"Oh. Oh shit, man, I . . ."

"With a burning tire around his neck, begging the rebels to let him live so he could raise his son. I was four years old."

"Oh my God. I . . . I mean—"

"So yes, ten minutes of talking to my only living relative on earth means a lot to me. More than you can ever imagine."

"Oh," I said quietly. I really wished I had something to do so I didn't have to focus on feeling like an asshole. This kid had reasons to be angry, reasons to be sad, probably reasons to kill himself. I was just a spoiled white kid with daddy issues.

We sat in silence for a minute. "Also," he said, "Chip knows how to hack the staff Wi-Fi and download porn onto an iPod. That might make an hour with the iPod more appealing."

I smiled. "Dude. I won't need more than fifteen seconds." And then he was smiling.

The next morning, I got woken up by a hand on my shoulder before the PA woke us up.

"What the hell?" I said.

"Get up," Mohammed told me.

"Why?"

"Because we've got to be on time all week for you to get your porn and me to get my phone call. We can't depend on any of these other people to take the lead, so it's up to you and me."

It was a real testament to how freaking tired I was that the prospect of access to forbidden porn wasn't enough to make me spring out of bed. It took Mohammed pouring water in my ear for that to happen. "Ah, what the hell?" I said, jumping out of bed.

"Get showered. We'll hit Chip's room before breakfast."

We wound up knocking on Chip's door only thirty seconds after the PA told all of Heartland to get out of bed.

Chip answered the door in his boxers with visible morning wood. Man, I hated this place. "What the hell do you guys want," he said, rubbing his eyes with one hand and trying to adjust the tentpole in his boxers with the other.

"We want to get a reward this week," Mohammed said. "It's important to us."

Chip looked at me, then Mohammed. "You told him about the porn, didn't you?" he said to Mohammed.

"It's not like you make it a secret," Mohammed said.

"Alright. I could use an hour with Xtube myself," Chip said. "Might make it easier to get through the week."

"Hey," I said. "I'm, uh, sorry about yesterday. I'm still pissed about being here, and—"

"Don't even worry about it, dude. You get a bunch of hotheads together, there's gonna be a scrap sooner or later. Just glad we got it out of the way early." He held out a fist. It wasn't the same hand that he just had on his junk, so I bumped it. And it was over.

This, sadly, was not the way girls rolled. Mohammed, Chip, and I were the first ones in the cafeteria, and Mohammed signaled to everybody from hothead group that we had to sit together. Diana, Emmy, and Jenny still weren't speaking to each other. No bacon on the menu today, but Diana was making a big deal out of eating her breakfast sausage and scrambled eggs, and Jenny looked like she was seriously considering hurting her.

I watched as Emmy took a single piece of honeydew melon and sliced it into twenty-five bite-sized pieces. She popped one in her mouth, chewed for ten seconds, swallowed, took a big gulp of water, and started on the next one.

"Really packing it away there, huh?" I said to her.

She looked up, hurt flashing across her eyes. "Be nice! It's just too much food for me all at once."

"Sorry. Reflex. You know, you get in the habit of being a dick, it's kind of hard to break it."

"Now that I wouldn't know about," Emmy said. Jenny snorted.

Emmy looked like she was about to say something back when Mohammed tapped a spoon on his plastic tumbler of orange juice. It made a dull clunking sound, and everybody stared at him. "Listen," he said. "I need my reward this week. My mom has been in Africa for the last three weeks, and I haven't spoken to her at all. I need to know what happened to my family. And we need to work together so we can—"

"Oh geez," Diana said. "The African guy has *problems*. Let's all do what the guards say so the guy with the *real* problems can get what he wants. Because *we're* not important."

I was thinking the same thing, but my desire for porn kept my mouth shut. "Diana. I have a thirty-two gig iPod. I've got *Goblet of Fire* on there. Daniel Radcliffe in the bathtub with his shirt off."

Diana looked at me. "Liar," she said.

"It's true," I said. "Sure would be nice to have an hour of iPod time, right?"

Diana stared at me, her little beady eyes boring into my skull. Finally she said, "Okay. I'm in."

I looked triumphantly at Chip and Mohammed. I'd successfully brought one of the toughest cases on board. So why were they looking at me like I was an idiot?

"Uh," Chip said. "Dude. If she's got your iPod, how are you going to—"

"Crap," I said, and Chip started laughing. "You can borrow mine. For ten minutes."

"And that's at least nine and a half more minutes than you're going to need," Mohammed whispered in my ear.

I laughed, and for a brief moment, things didn't seem so bad.

And then it was off to Aesthetics of Classic Film, which I thought might be okay, but today's class was just a lecture about silent movies. The teacher kept talking about *chiaroscuro*, which I thought was a sausage, though that didn't really make any sense in this context.

At least in Culinary Science we got to bake things, since that was about the only thing you could do in a kitchen without sharp knives, though we were told before the cookies came out of the oven that we could be proud that our classmates would get to enjoy them at dinner tonight.

"So we get to smell cookies baking and we don't get to eat them? The hell with that!" I yelled. I scooped up the pathetic remains of the batter with a rubber spatula from the bowl I was using and licked it. This would probably stop me from moving up a level, but it tasted great.

And then I had to have an emergency session with Max during which I explained that I really just wanted some cookies, and I wasn't trying to kill myself with salmonella from the uncooked eggs in the batter.

Which made me miss Fitness, which was fine with me. The terrors of the locker room could wait.

Then it was on to directed study time. I didn't have any homework to do, so I was instructed to write home.

Hey guys, I wrote. *Bars on the windows, bullshit classes, and rules about everything, including which way to wipe your butt. Front to back, in case you're wondering. Wish you were here. Instead of me.*

7.

EMMY

IN THE CAF THE NEXT MORNING, MOHAMMED TRIED ONCE AGAIN to keep us on track with the "all for one and one for all" setup Tina had instituted after the brawl by using a combo platter of intimidation and guilt. Everyone but me was totally fired up about the lame rewards, so they were perfectly happy to comply. Especially Justin, who seemed way more excited about watching gross actors have sex on a tiny little iPod screen than he was about having a real girl who might actually like him sitting right next to him.

As for me, I was so over it already. An hour of music or more talk time with my family just wasn't that motivating. If I could speak to Joss, sure, I would've been thrilled about the extension. But I wasn't allowed to chat with anyone other than my mom and dad until I got to level two, at which time I would have sup-posedly learned to "trust" again and started moving into the "realization" of how I had gotten myself into this predicament.

So things being the way they were, not only did I not want more time for that call to 'rents, I was totally dreading the awk-ward, guided conversation we were supposed to have during it. I'd been informed my goal for the required weekly report to Mom and Dad was to clearly and calmly communicate my progress in three key areas: Academic, therapeutic, and social. It was going to be totally weird, following a script like we were business associ-ates instead of people who actually knew each other. It seemed like just another way my parents were cutting ties with me. Even thinking about it hurt.

"I know I sort of agreed to this all at breakfast yesterday, but I decided last night there's nothing in this deal for me," I said, after gagging down five thousand bites of melon, scrambled eggs with spinach, and toast. I could practically feel cellulite forming on my thighs and ass as I chewed, and had to take deep breaths to make sure I didn't actually barf on anyone again—especially since the consequence for my unexpected puke was having a Staf-fie accompany me every time I went to the bathroom. I think the words Tina used when setting this up were, "We're onto you." So much for empathy from the therapists in this place.

"You know what's in it for you? Not pissing me off," Moham-med offered, the dark cloud that always seemed to be brewing around him bigger and more threatening than ever.

"Not a big motivator either. Sorry." I shot him a big smile to show how unafraid of him I was.

"Hey Emmy," Justin said, back to being his nice self and not the dickhead who'd mocked the way I ate and panted over the mere thought of porn. "I think I can make it worth your while."

"I doubt it, but try me."

"How about me, Mohammad, and Chip finish off the food you don't want to eat?" he said, tossing it off like it was no big deal, eliminating eight jillion calories from my daily intake. I would have cut off my arm to get this kind of perk. "Sound good, guys?"

They looked at each other, then back at me, and nodded.

"Tempting. But I'm not so sure we could make it work," I said, having to bite my tongue to keep from screaming *Yes! Yes! Yes!* My strategy: Play it cool and see if anyone was willing to up the ante. Might as well get as much out of my power position as possible.

"We'll make it work," Mohammed said, glancing around to make sure no one else was listening. "I've been here long enough to know when it's cool. Deal?"

"I really don't want to get caught . . ." I trailed off. And I really didn't. But I also didn't want to get fat again even more. Still, it wasn't as tough a call as I was making it out to be. It wasn't like I could go down any levels, and that being the case demerits were pretty meaningless.

Everyone stared around at each other, like *What do we do now?* Finally, Jenny started scribbling in her notebook. She hadn't spoken since those six little words in the puke group—*Wilbur was the coolest pig ever*—and based on the silence that filled our room all the time, I didn't expect her to anytime soon. When she'd finished writing, she ripped out the page and handed it to me.

I won't tell if you exercise in our room at night after lights-out.

That was part two of the consequence Tina had given me. After dinner most days, kids had the option of going to the rec center. Not me anymore, though, at least for the foreseeable future. No exercise plus bathroom supervision basically added up to hell on earth. And these guys had just given me an out.

I hesitated a second more, then totally caved. "Okay, you got me," I said, a goofy grin taking over my face.

Justin and Chip high-fived, Diana gave me the devil horns, and Jenny almost—almost—cracked a smile back at me. As for Mohammed, every time he knew no one important was look-ing, he knocked lightly on the table and I'd quickly shovel little mountains of food onto the boys' plates. Whenever I got rid of some eggs or a chunk of glistening buttered toast, an iota of mis-ery melted away with it. Sure, I was still left with the stubborn ache of loneliness and crappy knowledge that I'd been abandoned again. Hey, I'd take whatever small comfort I could get here.

Then it was off to class. Body Politics was first. I hadn't

noticed it before, but the room seemed divided into sections: Skinny-minnies on the right, chunky monkeys on the left. I chose a seat next to one of the skinny-minnies.

"You new here?" the girl asked me. She kind of reminded me of Joss with her freckles and blond ponytail. I mean, if Joss, who was an athlete, had been thirty pounds lighter. This girl had a total supermodel figure—giraffe legs, stick thin arms, flat belly and boobs, prominent collar bones. If she weren't being so friendly, I would've hated her for being so perfect.

"Is it that obvious?" I asked.

"That's kind of how it works," she explained. "Kids tend to hang out here based on what level they are. Most of the people around us are on levels one and two, with maybe a few threes thrown in. I'm Colbie, by the way. Level two. Been here a month now."

"How can you tell the kids over there are on the upper levels?" I imagined some sort of merit badge or pin I hadn't noticed yet.

Colbie gave me a knowing look, rolled her eyes, and puffed out her cheeks. I burst out laughing. "Are you kidding me? It's like a factory farm in this place," she explained. "They force-feed every-one who's the slightest bit thin until they get obscenely plump and juicy, and then you're kind of cooked, you know? They send you home so fat you don't want anyone to see you, so you never go out. And then your parents think you're totally fixed, like *Isn't that sweet! My teenager wants to spend Friday night on the couch watching movies me with me! Wasn't Heartland just so great for her?* And meanwhile, you're all like *Shoot me now, I'm a cow.*"

I scrunched up my nose. "So how can you stop it from happening?"

Colbie shrugged helplessly. "You can't! I've gained, like, ten pounds since I got here. I'm already a total heifer and it's just going to get worse!"

"Really?" I asked, horrified. Ten pounds in one month, times however many months kids got stuck here, had to be the scariest, meanest, most unfair punishment imaginable.

Colbie nodded sadly. "I mean, I'll do whatever I have to to get out, but the minute I get home, I'm on a starvation diet until all the weight comes off. Period, end of story."

I felt sorry for her and her inevitable porking out.

And happy for me that thanks to Justin, Mohammed, and Chip, I was going to be the only kid in the history of Heartland who managed to avoid becoming one of the factory farm girls on the other side of the room.

CHAPTER 8

JUSTIN

NOBODY KNEW WHO WAS GOING TO BLOW IT FOR US. BUT EVERYBODY knew somebody was. The only person who could be reasonably ruled out was Mohammed. He was really good—scarily good, actually—at keeping things under wraps. I guessed that was a skill you developed when you watched one of your parents murdered in front of your eyes.

So that left me, with my smart mouth and low tolerance for bullshit; Emmy, who couldn't stand food; Chip, who was at least as much of a dick as me, since we'd already thrown down once; Jenny, who was so fragile it was like she might crack and turn to a pitiful pile of dust at any second; and Diana, who was a violent psycho.

Of course, as Mohammed's three assault convictions showed,

he was kind of a violent psycho himself, and actually much scarier than Diana because he hid it better. Which meant there was no way I was mouthing off to some authority figure and risking sharing a room with a guy who knew revenge was a dish best served cold. And it got cold in the middle of the night out here in the heartland.

So, in the end, it was Diana, who probably figured as a thirteen-year-old girl who looked like a ten-year-old, she'd be most immune from Mohammed's revenge, that snapped. After an entire week with nobody getting in trouble, we could almost taste the upcoming rewards. And then, twenty minutes away from our deadline, Diana went apeshit in the cafeteria when she thought that someone cut in front of her in line. It took Tiny and one other similarly huge staff guy to restrain her.

Which meant everyone arrived at group in a really foul mood. Mohammed looked like he might kill somebody. I did not want to sit next to him, or really, within about a half mile of him. Neither, apparently, did anybody else, so he got the couch all to himself with the rest of us on beanbag chairs or, in my case, a hard plastic chair because Tina indicated that my sharing a beanbag chair with Emmy would be a no-no. Surprisingly, Emmy looked kind of bummed about that. Even more surprisingly, I kind of was, too.

"So," Tina said to start the group. "The first thing I want to say is that I don't want you guys to look at this as a failure."

Nobody said anything, though you could read "yeah, right, lady" on pretty much everyone's face.

"I mean, okay, you guys did not earn the reward you were after, but look at what you did accomplish. Justin, did you think at this time last week that you'd go a whole week without losing *any* points?"

I shrugged. "I guess not."

"Emmy, you've made tremendous progress this week." As if on cue, Chip let out a belch that was almost certainly fueled by the beef taco he scooped off of Emmy's tray when Mohammed knocked on the table.

"'Scuse me," Chip said, and Emmy looked like she was ready to take him down.

"And even Diana, who faced some challenges today, had her best week ever." Tina smiled at Diana. Diana scowled back.

Then Mohammed spoke. "I'm sorry, Tina, but it's really hard for me to hear about how these rich privileged kids had such great weeks, and all I want to do is talk to my mom to see if my cousins are still *alive*—"

"Now, I don't think I can allow you to—" Tina began.

"Will you put a fucking sock in it already?" Diana spat in Mohammed's direction. He looked scarier than he ever had and glowered at her. If this were a cartoon, there would have been a lit fuse coming out of the top of his head. "I mean, get the hell over yourself. You're always so goddamn self-righteous about how you have important problems and the rest of us are just spoiled rich kids. But here's the thing. You're here. You are at Heartland Academy, which is not cheap. Tina, do you guys give scholarships to this hellhole?"

"Well, you know, Heartland Academy strives to provide a really intense therapeutic—"

And Emmy cackled. "That means no!" she laughed.

"Right," Diana continued. "So somebody is fronting a hell of a lot of money to put your grumpy ass in that seat. So that 'I'm just a poor African thing' is bullshit. I bet you there are people still in whatever toilet you come from who have to just live with the shit they saw and don't get a high-priced therapeutic setting to work out their issues. Right? So who the hell are you to judge anybody?"

I looked to Tina, who really ought to have put a stop to this. I was kind of afraid that Mohammed was going to kill Diana. But Tina just put on her "I'm a concerned, but disinterested party to this dispute" face, and we all stared at Mohammed.

"How I am able to be here is none of your—"

"Yeah, but see, it is our business," Diana said. "Because you're happy to throw your personal business in our faces as long as it makes you feel better than us. But now you want some privacy? Please."

Mohammed glowered some more. He clenched and unclenched his fists. He closed his eyes and breathed deeply.

Jenny not-too-subtly scooted her chair a few inches away from him. But Diana looked him right in his closed eyes, daring him to snap. It was like she actually wanted to throw down.

Mohammed had four years, ten inches, and probably eighty pounds on Diana, and yet I really didn't know who I would pick to win.

"Ten bucks on Diana," Emmy whispered to me.

"You're on," I said. I had just bet on a seventeen-year-old boy to beat up a thirteen-year-old girl. I suspected this was probably wrong.

Fortunately I didn't have to face down the issue of feeling bad for winning ten bucks on an uneven fight or, you know, losing ten bucks, because this was where Tina stepped in. "Diana, we've all got a right to keep some things private. Nobody has any obligation to disclose their financials to you. And you," she said, gesturing at Mohammed, "I am so proud of you. I can see how angry you are right now, and I just—you have made so much progress since you got here, and I just want you to know that I see that and honor it."

Tina's eyes were moist. I rolled my eyes and caught Emmy's eyes, which were also rolling. Nobody said anything for a minute. Which stretched into two. Which stretched into five, and then it was really, really awkward.

Tina was the first one to break the silence. "So," Tina said. "We've got another thirty minutes. Do you guys want to say anything, or are we just going to sit here?"

"I wanna play a game!" Diana said, and everybody groaned, probably picturing a torturous round of Sorry or Monopoly.

"Well, Diana, what game would you like to play?"

"The ass game!"

"Uh, Diana, I'm not sure what that is, but I don't think—"

"Substitute ass for heart in any song title. Go!" She pointed at Emmy.

"Um. 'Achy Breaky Ass'?" I laughed at that one, as did Chip, but nobody else was impressed.

Tina sputtered, "Emmy, please, the language—"

"'Ass of Stone'!" Chip piped in. Crickets.

"I don't know American music," Mohammed said.

"Jenny?" Diana said. "Not talkin', huh? Okay, you get a song Kanye West wrote about Emmy. 'Assless.'"

Everybody, even Emmy and Mohammed, laughed at that one. Tina was still offering feeble protests, but now it was in full swing, and we were all shouting titles out. "'Assbeat'!" "'Ass-Shaped Box'!" "'Jar of Asses'!" "'Stereo Asses'!" "'Ass-break Hotel'!"

And finally Tina had had enough. She stood up, red-faced, and yelled, "All of you! Stop it right now! Now, I'm sorry you had a disappointment this week, but that doesn't mean you get to flout every rule at Assland—Heartland Academy!"

Nobody said anything for a second. And then Diana piped up with, "Assland Academy? Tina, that is genius! Assland!"

"No, guys, listen, I misspoke with the—" Tina tried to protest, but everybody was laughing so loud and hard she couldn't get her sentence out.

"Assland Academy," Chip said, "a Caring Place!"

"Nestled in the Ass of America, Assland Academy provides a therapeutic setting . . . " Emmy added.

"Nestled in the ass!" I panted between laughs. "Good one! Tina, this is a winner! I haven't laughed this hard since I got to Assland!"

Tina waited patiently, blushing, until we stopped laughing. It took awhile.

"Okay, guys. I'm not knocking you down a level for this because I'm happy that you got through your rough time, and, apart from Diana's Kanye West remark, none of it was really abusive—"

"Have you seen this girl?" Diana asked. "It's just accurate."

Emmy shrugged. "True. Even when I was a tub I never had much of a butt."

Tina nodded. "Great. Anyway, I want to give you guys another chance to work together." She offered us a double-or-nothing deal. Two hours with the iPods and twenty extra minutes on the phone for another week of good behavior. I looked around the circle and saw the wheels turning in everyone's mind. What could I do with the extra time? Did last week's deals still hold, or were we in new territory here?

All was answered at dinner. "So last week's deals are still in effect," Mohammed said when everybody had brought their tray back to the table.

"No way," Diana said. "I want to renegotiate." I'd give the kid this. She had balls of steel. I was also happy because if she wanted to renegotiate, that was gonna give me two hours with the iPod. I had a semi just thinking about it.

It wasn't Mohammed who stepped in to keep her in line, though. It was Emmy. "As the person who blew the original deal, you're not really in the position to dictate terms."

"Yeah, actually I am," Diana said. "Because a) I started the ass game that resulted in the greatest name for this place ever. And b) I don't care. I'll go off right now and wreck the whole week for all of you. I don't care. So you have to make me care. And Daniel Radcliffe isn't enough. I want out."

Everybody looked around. "Out," Chip said. "You want to escape? To go where? You gonna go live in a cornfield?"

Diana took a big bite of her sloppy joe. The red goo oozed from between her lips, and Emmy looked totally green, like she might just barf right here and wreck it for us. "Close your eyes, for God's sake!" I yelled at Emmy. She did, putting her palms down on the table and taking deep breaths.

"Mmm . . ." Diana said with a mouth full of beef and bread. "I really like the way the beef fat mixes with the tomato. Mmmfh. And after you chew and mix it with your saliva, it makes this hot slurry of—"

It was clearly touch and go with Emmy right then. "I really like to exercise," I said, hoping to plant a reassuring image in her mind. "Just hit the treadmill for an hour and a half or so. You know, my treadmill's broken, though, and it only tells me how many calories I'm burning in a minute. So, Emmy, if I can run at a pace that allows me to consistently burn six calories a minute—"

"Then you're obviously not running fast enough, lazy," Emmy said. And everybody laughed, and Diana's evil spell was broken.

"Listen," Mohammed said through clenched teeth. "If we get our rewards two more weeks in a row, we'll get a field trip anyway. You don't have to break out to get off campus."

Diana chewed on this information and her sloppy joe. "I don't care. I can't wait two weeks. I'll lose it. I mean, I'm losing it already. I need some fresh air. Look at this place—" She gestured around at our subterranean dining hall, with the high windows covered in wire mesh and the ancient green-and-white linoleum squares on the floor, and it was easy to see what she meant. "I can't breathe in here. You guys help me break out, I'll be an angel until then."

"Do we have to come with you?" Chip asked. "Because then you're basically asking us to never ever get out of here. You know breaking out shows that you still have to work on your issues with authority, that you're not taking responsibility for your own actions—"

"That you're still blaming others for your own bad decisions," Emmy piped in.

"That you can't see it's not that the world is against you, it's that you are against the world," Chip said. "And you haven't achieved balance and wholeness."

"Yeah, I'm really not supposed to be here anyway," I said. "The whole thing was a misunderstanding. So I am damn sure not signing up for more time in this place just so you can go play *Children of the Corn*."

"What the hell is that?" Diana asked.

"It's a horror movie about psychotic kids," I said. "I think you'd identify." And Diana was up off the bench and ready to come over the table at me.

"Fifty bucks on Diana," Emmy said, laughing, as Chip restrained Diana and got her back in her seat.

Mohammed gave me a look. And then he spoke. "Fine," he said. "We'll break you out. *After* you behave for a week." He extended his hand, and Diana reached out and shook it.

I should have been happy that I had something to look forward to. When I'd gotten into my bed, I had a smile on my face.

And then I woke up in the morning, and something was wrong. My head wasn't right.

I stumbled through academic classes, including Fitness, which turned out to involve walking around the track out back.

And then it was Max time.

"How are you doing today?" he said.

I'd been resisting Max pretty effectively up until now—giving him glib sarcasm as much as possible and never saying anything meaningful. But today I didn't have the fight left. This, of course, was how they got you.

"I'm numb," I said.

Max looked up from his iPad. "Physically?" he said.

"No. Just emotionally. You know. I just don't feel anything."

"Why do you think that is?"

They always asked this question. And it always pissed me off. I didn't know why. I mean, my parents were divorced, but that just made me like about half the kids in America. I had a pretty good life.

"There is no reason, Max," I said. "That's why this is a waste of time. Because we can talk and talk and talk and we'll never figure out why I'm screwed up. It's just the way my brain works. Or doesn't work. Sometimes I just start feeling numb, and then after that it gets painful, and I don't know why. I can't figure out why now, after I had the best day I ever had at this hellhole, I suddenly get numb."

"You haven't been palming the meds or anything, have you?"

I'd been on a low dose of Citalopram, the cheapest antidepressant, since the acetaminophen incident. It helped. But not enough. I rolled my eyes. "I'm taking my medicine."

"Well," Max said. "So you don't want to talk about causes. Fine. Then let's focus on strategies. If you're headed into a rough patch, how do you get through it?"

"I don't know. I mean, that's why I'm here, isn't it?"

Max smiled at me like I'd made some kind of breakthrough.

"Okay. So tell me what it's like."

"I mean. It's like. I don't feel anything for a while. Not happy, not sad. Like, my AM group might get a field trip or whatever if we're all good for two weeks, and I'm not looking forward to it. I just don't feel anything right now. It's not bad. But it's not good."

"Okay," Max said, tapping frantically on his iPad and nearly salivating at the therapeutic breakthrough he thought we were having. "So then what?"

"Then, when the numbness goes away, the pain hits."

"And then what?"

"And then . . . well. I get mean. I alienate people. And I do stupid things."

"You gonna do that stuff here?"

"You got another idea for me? Because, and you know how much it kills me to say this, I am actually pretty open right now."

Max stroked his Old Testament beard for a minute. "The thing is," he finally said, "it has to come from you. I can't tell you how to get through it because it's different for everybody."

"Awesome. Now I see why they pay you the big bucks around here," I said.

The next day I was still numb, and I probably wouldn't have

gotten out of bed except I knew if I so much as missed breakfast I'd blow it for everybody and Mohammed would beat the snot out of me. Not that I was too concerned about that. I mean . . . I wasn't afraid of it. In fact I kind of wondered if it might be worth it just to feel something. I decided to leave that option for another day. I hopped in the shower and shuffled down to breakfast, where Emmy was doing an autopsy on a slice of honeydew.

"No smartass thing to say about my breakfast?" she asked, smiling.

I put a spoonful of something in my mouth. It didn't taste like anything. "I'm too numb to be my usual sparkling self," I said. "You know, the numbness?"

Emmy chewed a sliver of honeydew twenty-seven times and looked at me. "No. I don't get that. What's it like?"

"It's like nothing. Like I just feel totally flat."

"Like, sad? I have crying jags."

"Nope. Not sad. Just nothing."

She picked up another sliver of honeydew with her fork and chewed it twenty-seven times. "Doesn't sound so bad," she finally said. "You want my bacon? I obviously have to get rid of it before Jenny gets down here."

"Not really. But you know Chip will be all over it."

"Yeah. So how long does it last? The feeling nothing, not your hatred of bacon."

I cracked a weak smile. "Depends. A day, a week, a month? I

don't know. I don't really mind. It's better than the pain, which usually comes after. You know, when you have this feeling in your guts like it just hurts to be alive?"

Emmy pointed her fork—which sported another seven molecules of melon on the end—at me. "Now that one," she said, "I'm totally familiar with."

Last time I felt that way I'd taken a lot of Tylenol. Which didn't really help. Obviously. But I thought, you know, painkillers. Didn't kill the pain, though. But then the pain just kind of left on its own a couple of weeks later. I didn't know why.

I kept hearing Max's question. "How do you get through it?"

He was asking about my latest downturn, but I guessed the question could apply to life, too. And I didn't know the answer.

9.

EMMY

TWO DAYS A WEEK, INSTEAD OF STUDY HALL I WENT TO A ONE-ON-one session with my assigned therapist. I'd only met with her twice so far, and had spent the entire time trying to convince her my admission to Heartland was all a big mistake.

It totally didn't work, but I figured it couldn't hurt to keep trying.

"So how how is it going this week? Are you adjusting to being away from home and getting used to the rules here at Heartland?" Brittany was asking me.

Brittany seemed like a better name for a sorority sister than a therapist. She looked like a college kid, too, with her perfectly cut bangs and perky boobs. Her age and hotness made me fairly certain I would eventually outsmart her.

"It hasn't been a problem at all for *me*," I said, emphasizing that I wasn't the one with issues.

My words just hung out there as Brittany nodded, unblinking. I figured she wasn't picking up on what I was laying down, so I gave her a little hint. "I mean, I appreciate the structure that Heartland provides and it's been a real eye-opener. I understand now that my mom was pretty concerned about me not eating as healthfully as I should have been, and posting mean things about a classmate."

Brittany smiled encouragingly. This was going to be so easy, it was laughable. "And I really think I've learned my lesson and I'm ready to go home. But Tina has me tethered to a pretty messed-up group—"

Brittany raised an eyebrow.

"I'm sorry, I know that sounded mean. But it's just that these kids seem to have way bigger problems than just making poor eating choices and using Facebook inappropriately. And I really feel like they're impeding my progress. So do you think we could come up with a mutually acceptable release plan, preferably by the end of this month so I can pursue my dream of attending Simon's Rock this academic year?"

Brittany looked at me so sweetly I thought for sure I was golden. Until she came back with this. "Do you think you could cut the bullshit for a second so we can talk about what's really going on with you?"

I noticed the familiar rumblings in my stomach, a mix of starvation and pissed-off-edness that sometimes threatened to double me over. "I'm offended that you think I'm full of . . . *merde*," I said, using the French word for "shit" so I wouldn't get any demerits, even though the swearing rule didn't seem to apply here in Brittany's office. Or Tina's group, for that matter.

"Well, that makes us even. Because I'm offended you underestimate me so much you'd think I would fall for that crap you just handed me. Want one?" she asked, holding out a box of graham crackers.

I performed a quick mental calculation and, deciding I could do an extra ten minutes of jogging in place after lights-out, took one. I broke the two squares in half, put one on my lap and proceeded to break the other into four smaller pieces. I put the first little square in my mouth and let it sit there, the sugary goodness melting on my tongue until the sharp edges of the cracker turned mushy and round. My head buzzed pleasantly.

"I love these," Brittany said, crunching down on an entire cracker and swallowing it in record time. I wondered how she stayed so thin, and considered warning her against eating too many before deciding it wasn't worth the risk. She'd figure it out on her own when her pants didn't button anymore.

"Me too," I said, putting the next small piece in my mouth. This time, it clung to the roof of my mouth like dried bird shit. I grabbed for my water bottle and took a big gulp. The cracker went halfway down and got stuck. I chugged some more and the lump finally dissolved.

Brittany grabbed another cracker. The number of calories she was consuming in one sitting was way more than I'd ever allow myself. "So how long have you been struggling with an eating disorder?" she asked, like it was a totally normal, polite thing to say.

"I haven't," I said, inhaling crumbs, which sent me into a coughing fit. "Ever."

"Well then, what about the anger? How long has that been building?"

"I don't know why everyone assumes I'm angry," I said once I'd stopped hacking, even more pissed off about this question than the eating one. Cracker number three went into Brittany's mouth and down her gullet. I was horrified, but tried not to let it show.

"I'd say posting more than fifty vicious comments about someone on Facebook in a single week would indicate you're a pretty angry person."

Not this again. When was everyone going to let that go? I was absolutely not getting into the nitty-gritty details of why I'd done that, especially to an adult. No way, no how. "That boy yelled racist remarks at me every single time I walked by him in the hall. I mean, who wouldn't be pissed off?" I slapped my hand on my leg for emphasis and cracker went flying everywhere. "Sorry.

I mean, I guess you could say I'm situationally angry. But I definitely wouldn't classify myself as an angry person."

Brittany stood up and stretched. "I get the feeling me asking you questions isn't going to get us anywhere today, so why don't we try something a little different instead? Come on."

I followed her down the hall to a tiny closet filled floor to ceiling with little knick-knacks and Polly Pockets and McDonald's toys. "Uh, Brittany? I grew out of playing with dolls when I was seven."

Brittany waved me into the closet as she stepped out of it. It was too tight a space for us to both fit in there at once. "Think of it as an experiment in your unconscious. Just pick out anything that speaks to you in any way, put it all in this basket, and then meet me back in my office."

She left me staring at a plethora of babyish figurines. As much as I had no interest in her game, I knew I wasn't getting out of it, so I started tossing things randomly into the basket. Animals, Disney characters, whatever. Who cared, right? I was way too smart to fall for talking about my problems while playing dolly.

When I got back to Brittany's office, she had a miniature sandbox set up on the coffee table. I felt like I was back in preschool, when all the kids used to ask me why my my skin was a different shade than theirs, and one mean boy even pulled his eyelids tight every day to try and look like me.

"You can't be serious," I said, looking from my basket of dolls to the sandbox to Brittany.

"Sure I can," she said, as calm and reassuring as ever. "So just set everything up in here any way that feels right to you and we can talk about it after."

"Seriously?" I asked again. I couldn't believe she was using on me what was clearly a therapy thing for kids with zero verbal skills.

Brittany just nodded and pointed at the sandbox.

I sighed and grabbed the first thing that found its way into my hand: A pink elephant with an elaborate painted-on headdress. I buried him in the middle of the sandbox, so only his trunk was showing. Next I found Mulan dressed in warrior gear and put her in a corner. Then I took this Nordic king and queen and placed them in the opposite corner. Finally, I pulled out Alice in Wonderland and put her next to Mulan, figuring Mulan looked like she could use a good girlfriend.

But something stopped me from feeling like I was done. The sandbox just didn't look right at all. I was telling myself not to be ridiculous even as I moved Alice over to where the Norse king and his wife stood. "There," I finally said.

"So tell me about the scene you've created here, Emmy."

I stared down at the preschool portrait. "It's a bunch of toys in a sandbox."

Brittany laughed. "Come on, smartass. Humor me."

"Okay, fine," I said, smiling back at her despite myself. Oddly, I liked how she didn't let me get away with shit. It felt like a challenge. "In this corner, Mulan. And in the blue cape, her opposition . . . ummmm . . . Thor!"

Brittany gave me a little wink. "Go on. You're a natural at this."

"Anyway, this is war. Mulan versus Thor and Thor's wife. It's going to be an epic battle where the cards are stacked against Mulan, but I think she'll come out on top."

"What about her?" Brittany asked, pointing at Alice in Wonderland.

"She's the beautiful ring girl," I said, pleased at my quick wit.

Brittany picked up Mulan and handed her to me. "So what can you tell me about Mulan?"

"Well, for one thing, she's Chinese," I said, and all of a sudden I had a sinking feeling this kid's game was going to get me to reveal a hell of a lot more than I'd intended to. So maybe I wasn't so smart after all.

"Right," Brittany said, thankfully not stating the obvious. "What else do you know about her?"

"Well . . . she loves her family and wants to protect them. She hides who she really is from almost everybody. And she's tough and courageous and fights back hard against the big bad guys even though she's just a little girl . . ."

"Kind of like you, right?" Brittany said.

I nodded, because I couldn't really think of a believable way to deny it.

"Did you notice that Alice in Wonderland wanted to be with Mulan, but you couldn't let her? You made her leave?" Brittany continued analyzing my toy story.

I could clearly see what was unfolding here—that Mulan was me, Alice was supposed to be Joss, and Thor and his wife were my mom and dad—but there was nowhere to run and hide. "I guess," I said, my voice barely a whisper.

"What might that mean?" she asked gently.

"That Joss actually *wants* to hang out with me? Like, she doesn't just feel sorry for me or pity me or something?"

Brittany did me the favor of not looking smug about me admitting this. I appreciated it more than she would ever know. "Now look at Thor and his wife. Do they really look like they want to fight with Mulan, or hurt her in any way?"

I picked up the big, burly blond guy and his wife and stared at them more closely. When I hastily chose them back in the closet, I was totally positive they looked mean and mad. But now, in this light, Thor looked more concerned than anything, and his wife just looked plain old sad. "No," I muttered. "They look worried, I guess. And maybe scared."

"So do you think maybe your parents sent you here because they love you and are extremely concerned about you? And that maybe the only person you're fighting is yourself?"

I shrugged, those tears that always seemed to be waiting just below the surface shimmering in my eyes. I bit my lip and tried to hold it together.

"What about this guy here?" Brittany asked, pointing to the buried elephant.

"He's..." I started, my voice shaky and small. "He's hoping no one can see the obvious, I guess. That he's there and looks kind of unusual."

"So tell me everything you know about elephants," Brittany said.

"Well, for one thing, they're very sensitive and have strong emotions. And um... they're revered for their strength and wisdom in Asian cultures. Also, they mourn the loss of their family members forever..." I trailed off, knowing what was coming next.

"That sounds a lot like you, too, doesn't it Emmy?"

I nodded. It was mortifying, but I couldn't hold back my tears any longer. Brittany gathered me into a hug and I buried my head into her awesome-smelling sorority girl hair.

"We'll get to the bottom of all of this, Emmy. I promise. You're not alone, okay? We're all here for you. Me, Alice in Wonderland, Thor, and his wife—even the five people Tina has you tethered to."

And I couldn't help but laugh a little even as I sobbed on Brittany's shoulder.

CHAPTER 10

JUSTIN

THE WEEK ENDED WITHOUT INCIDENT AND, AS PROMISED, WE ALL got our rewards. I was still a little bit numb, so I wasn't as excited about the whole thing as I thought I'd be, but I did enjoy the iPod time. It was safe to say everybody got a little more relaxed as a result. Well, almost everybody. Mohammed had to wait until Sunday night to make his phone call to see who was alive, though I still wasn't clear on that whole thing—like, he got a ten-minute phone call last week; what was magic about the twenty-minute phone call?

Mine sure as hell wasn't magic. Just Mom telling me the usual stuff about what was happening at home, which aunt wasn't speaking to which other aunt, and stuff like that. It wasn't all that interesting, and I didn't have anything to add to the conversation.

Because what was happening here that I could tell her about? "Well, guess what, Mom? Sexual Reactivity group is still really awkward. No breakthrough in my one-on-one sessions yet. And the whole Anger Management group is getting together to break out and probably lose all our privileges for the rest of the school year." Yeah. So I didn't say much. And Mom cried. And I felt bad.

I didn't start crying until after I hung up. Then I slumped down in the phone booth, grabbed my knees, and let it go.

So here was the pain I knew was coming right behind the numbness. Fantastic. The first time this happened, I was diagnosed with clinical depression. The second time I took a fistful of Tylenol, which might be a good name for an action movie with a depressed or possibly arthritic hero.

I didn't know what it felt like for other people with this diagnosis. For me it was like somebody squeezing my stomach with a cold iron fist. Except it wasn't really a physical pain. It was just like the act of being alive hurt so freaking much that if anybody touched me I thought I might shatter into a million pieces.

And this brittle feeling was really closely related to the anger. Because when you're in constant pain, people who aren't in pain were really annoying. And people asking you to do stuff you didn't want to do were even more annoying. Like, really, why the hell would you ask me to take out the garbage when it took every freaking ounce of my energy just to feign normalcy while I was sitting here?

So, yeah, hence the anger issues. Although, I could be a dick even when I wasn't in pain, so who knew.

I guess I just didn't feel like anything was helping me here. Max, who was supposed to be the linchpin or keystone or something important in my "circle of support," though circles don't have one part that holds the whole thing together, said I had to figure stuff out for myself. Awesome. This place sucked.

So I just curled up on the floor of the old-fashioned phone booth they made us use for our calls. It was really cool to be in this relic from another century, but the best part about it was that I could be alone. I mean, even doors to the bathroom stalls here were pretty low and sported a large gap where the door met the frame, so the staff could check in on us at any time. But here in the phone booth, even though the doors had panes of glass, it was quiet and solitary and it smelled like wood and it felt good. I really could have stayed there all day. And it crossed my mind, but then there was a knock on the door, and Mohammed opened it up.

"Your twenty's up," he said. "My turn." I wiped my eyes with my sleeve, snorked back a big gob of crying-induced snot, and slid out of the phone booth. I wanted to go up to my room and lie down, but I couldn't face the stairs right then. Pathetic. I headed toward the lounge, which might have been nice when the shabby couches and chairs were bought, I was guessing sometime in the mid-nineties. As I walked away from the phone booth, I could swear I heard Mohammed say, "Hey, baby," as he closed the door. Who the hell called their mom "baby"? Well, I guess if he didn't have issues, he wouldn't be here.

Chip was sitting on a ratty couch in the lounge with a netbook on his lap. The walls were painted this warm shade of yellow, but there was nothing on them. Two kids were playing chess at the long wooden table that sat about five feet in front of the couch. There was no TV for it to block. Three kids were actually playing Sorry. Like they were eight or something, not in high school like we all were here.

I didn't feel like talking, but I did feel that I should express my gratitude to Chip if I ever wanted to get access to his Internet genius again.

"Hey, Chip," I said. "Thanks for the, uh, hookup."

Chip gave me a big smile. "No problem," he said. "Hey, I'm working on a paper," Chip continued. "You wanna read it?" I looked at him like he was insane. Well. More so.

"It's a really good paper," Chip said to me.

He was giving me a look that said there was more going on here than I thought, so I said, "Alright, cool."

Over his shoulder, I could see that Chip had the web browser open, and he was looking through what were clearly everybody's Assland intake records. I had no idea how he got this, but with a couple of clicks, he navigated to a page that was very interesting. "Whoa," I said. "Fascinating paper indeed."

"Yeah," Chip said. "It certainly is." Knowledge was power, and power was something we had very little of in this place, so it should have made me really happy to have this little nugget of knowledge about one of my classmates. But I was too deep in the hole of my depression. All it did was make me angry.

Monday morning I was the second one to breakfast, so I went to sit next to Emmy, who was doing her daily honeydew autopsy. "You don't have to," she said, and I just looked at her. "We already got our reward. And I'm guessing you enjoyed yours a lot more than you will sitting here with me."

"Um. But *can* I sit here with you?" I could hear my voice sounding kind of angry. I mean, it wasn't like we were besties, and I might have hassled her about her food stuff. But I still kind of liked Emmy, and it pissed me off that she didn't seem to like me much today.

"No offense," she said (which translates to "here comes something offensive"), "but I would like to sit alone and have some quiet time this morning. It's all been a little intense, you know?"

"I have no idea what the hell you're talking about, but I won't bug you with my presence," I said, and I grabbed the edges of my tray so tightly that I kind of wondered if I was gonna snap it in two. I was just about to walk away when a small hand on my shoulder shoved me into a seat.

"Don't even think about it," Diana said. "We have to start planning. Operation Free Bird is almost ready to launch, and we have to make sure it goes off without a hitch."

"Well, I'm sorry, but Emmy wants to dissect her melon in peace," I said.

Diana gritted her teeth and sat right next to me. "I don't care what the hell she wants," Diana said. "You owe me. You all owe me. And unless I get out *this week*, the staff is going to know all about your"—she pointed a spoon loaded with Lucky Charms and milk at Emmy—"food dumps and extra exercise, and *your*"—and this time the spoon of destiny pointed in my direction—"disgusting perversions. So let's get planning," she said.

Emmy looked at me, presumably to share the "can you believe this kid" moment, but I had my eyes on my Grape Nuts. The hell with her.

Diana waited until Chip and Mohammed trickled into the cafeteria and sat down, then talked in a quiet (and, therefore, coming from her kind of scary) voice.

"So here's what I want," she said. "It's Monday. And this" — she looked from side to side and unfolded a state fair flyer on the table for us to look at—"starts this weekend. So you've got five days to figure out how to get us there."

The general consensus was that Diana's idea was completely crazy, and it wasn't going to happen. Then Diana made similar threats to Chip and Mohammed that she already made to Emmy and me. Still nobody came up with a solution by the end of breakfast.

I was in a crappy mood already, and now this tiny tyrant was going to ruin everybody's life. I mean, I felt like I was just getting the hang of how to handle Assland, and now one way or the other, it was getting screwed up on Friday. Awesome.

So, yeah, I wasn't in the best mood for Sexual Reactivity group, and then we opened group with Jack looking at me through his John Lennon specs and saying, "So, Justin, you've been lurking for a couple of weeks now. I think it's time for you to explain why you think you're here."

I rolled my eyes and appealed to the rest of the group for some help. Not that I was really expecting any. They all looked at me like, *You think you're so much better than us. Let's hear what you got.* Or, anyway, that was how I imagined it.

"Fine," I spit out. "Here we go. It's a short story. Memorial Day weekend. Met a girl at the amusement park. Brought her home, or anyway, to the place where my dad lives, which isn't my home, he's got all his workout junk in the room that's supposed to be mine, and I have to crash on the pullout couch, but whatever. Anyway, so she goes down on me, Dad walks in. That's the whole story. Now do you guys get why I don't really think this group is appropriate for me?"

"What was the girl's name?" Jack, the facilitator whose last name was probably not really Inghoff, said.

"Kristin? Caitlyn? I guess there's an outside chance it was Kitten. Anyway, something with a 'kuh' at the beginning and an 'en' at the end."

"How long had you been going out?" some kid named Troy asked.

"Well, we weren't really going out. I mean, I had only met her a couple of hours earlier."

"And how's her summer been going?" another kid, Brent, chimed in.

"How the hell do I know? I barely even knew her! Okay? So what? I mean, listen to you guys—not that I'm judging anyone else's issues, God forbid, though that's exactly what you assholes are doing to me, I guess it's okay as long as I'm not the one doing it, huh, Jack? But I mean, one blow job! Does that qualify me for this group? I mean, I don't even agree with the idea of this group! Sex isn't bad!"

Jack pushed his glasses back on his nose, took a deep breath, and said, "Of course sex isn't bad, Justin. And while it's true that you don't have the range of experience that most people here have, I don't think your behavior is exactly healthy."

"It's not healthy to be interested in sex at age sixteen? Then I guess pretty much everybody is unhealthy."

"Here's what's not necessarily healthy—being sixteen and having sex with someone you just met."

"We didn't have sex, I told you. She just—"

"Oral sex is sex, Justin. Hence the name. And, yeah, you're right, sex with someone you just met is not the riskiest thing you could do, but it is risky behavior. And sex with someone you don't care about is—like, if you weren't doing this because you care about it, why were you doing it?"

"Well, I guess she was doing it to get back at her boyfriend."

"And what about you?"

"What about me?"

"Why were you doing it?"

"What the hell kind of stupid question is that? Because it feels fucking awesome to have a girl's mouth on your dick!" I really wanted to throw something. As it was, I had my fists clenched, and if I'd had any nails, they would have been digging into my palms.

Jack looked at me for a minute, then turned to the group. "Okay, Justin, thank you for sharing. Now how about you, Troy?"

I sat and fumed for the rest of the stupid group. What the hell were they doing to us here anyway? I mean, the admittedly short amount of time I'd spent with Caitl—or Krist—in was the only time in the last six months when I'd felt good, when it felt like everything was working. I didn't even mean that in a pervy way. I just meant I felt like I was fine being me and things were kind of okay. And Assland wanted to take that away from me. Now I was supposed to go back and feel guilty about it or, like, the only time I felt like a normal healthy kid was actually unhealthy. *Sorry, Justin, but you'll never get it right. That time you thought you were happy? Wrong!*

My fury didn't really go away for the rest of the day. Even though I was figuring out how to navigate the million rules, all this place had done so far was make me feel worse. Diana's idea about breaking out seemed way less crazy than it had before SR group. I mean, sure, they were gonna catch us eventually—we were in the middle of nowhere, after all—but at least we'd be in control of something. For a really short period of time, we would be one hundred percent in charge of our whereabouts and activities—nobody telling us what to do, and nobody telling us that what we were doing or thinking or wanting was wrong.

I was the last one to get to the dinner table, and before I even said hi to everybody, I looked Diana in the eye and said, "I'm in. I don't care if it's just you and me. I'm in."

II.

EMMY

"IT'S NEVER GOING TO WORK. WHY DON'T YOU JUST GIVE IT UP?" I whispered to Diana before Anger Management group started.

The crew's whole "breakout" plan was so ridiculous. There was nothing "out there"—meaning the immediate surroundings of Assland—interesting enough to do such a pointless thing. They were never going to make it to the fair, which was at least ninety miles from here. Without a doubt, they'd be hauled back sooner rather than later. I just didn't get the appeal.

And I mean, I didn't like being watched all the time, or told what to eat and when to sleep, or getting judged by teachers and therapists as to whether I was making adequate progress any more than Justin and Diana did. But the alternative they were proposing was what? Playing in a cornfield for a few minutes?

Sneaking into the hayloft of some farmer's barn and hiding out there for a couple of hours? No thanks. Assland was better than exile in No Man's Land.

"What's never going to work?" Tina asked as she bustled into the room.

Diana shook her head and squinted at me. I shrugged, like, *Go ahead, tell her.*

"Emmy's plan to lose more weight," Diana announced. "Which, can I say, is really stupid since she's already practically nonexistent."

"What about your plan, Diana? Care to share that with Tina?" I shot back at her.

Mohammed clenched and unclenched his fists rhythmically. Chip gave me a warning look. Justin ignored everyone and Jenny sat there mute as ever.

"And what plan is that, Diana?" Tina asked, leaning forward in her "ready to listen pose," which made me crazy. It was like we could say anything to her—*I just sacrificed twelve squirrels to the devil! I shoved a D battery up my ass and boy does it feel good!*— and she'd still have that same calm demeanor.

Diana opened and closed her mouth a few times before this finally came out. "My plan to kick Emmy's scrawny little ass the next time she dumps food on my plate and expects me to eat it."

I yelped. There was no way Diana was going to ruin this for me. Not when I'd finally worked out the whole food thing so I wouldn't join Alisha and the factory farm girls on their side of Body Politics class.

Tina raised an eyebrow at me. "Is that true, Emmy?"

I tried to match Tina's pleasant tone of voice and expression even though I was about ready to lose it. "It's only as true as Diana's plan to get us to bust her out of here," I said sweetly. If Diana was going to get my secret reward taken away from me, I was sure as hell going to do the same to her.

Tina's la-la-dippy-happy look morphed into a super-concerned one. "And is that true, Diana?"

Diana's face was so red by this point it seemed like it might just melt right off her body. "No!" she yelled.

Tina looked around the group. "Do any of you know anything about Emmy not getting proper nutrition or Diana plotting to leave campus?"

More shrugs, a bunch of shaking heads.

Tina clasped her hands together. "Okay, I got it. No one wants to rat anyone out. That's progress, too! You're finally learning to work together as a group, even if it is possibly protecting some not-so-healthy plans and actions."

Justin pretended to sneeze but instead of "Achoo!" out came "Bullshit!"

"Do you have something to say, Justin?"

I knew he had depression and was currently in a bad place, but it was kind of amazing how much energy he put into being mad. Like, most of the time lately he moved in slow motion and had no desire to do anything—well, except maybe watch porn—and then suddenly something little would make his head nearly pop off.

"Yeah I have something to say. This is all such bullshit. You're acting like we're making some big-ass breakthroughs. The truth is, we only give a shit about what *acting* like we give a shit about each other is going to get us. And the really stupid part is, none of this helps anyone, no matter how hard you try to pretend like it does."

Tina nodded calmly through Justin's tirade. "Great observations, Justin. Thanks for sharing such honest emotions with us."

Justin's face contorted into a scary mask. "That's just the kind of thing I'm talking about! I don't feel any better, but no matter what I say or how I say it, you act like you've given me the key to happiness!"

Tina nodded some more. I'm sure some part of Justin wanted to wring her neck, but the outburst seemed to have taken a lot out of him. He was back to bonelessness. "I understand your feelings of frustration, Justin. I also understand that the structure of Heartland sometimes makes students acutely miss their independence."

Chip snorted. "You could say that."

The sarcastic remark only got Tina more into it. "So let's explore this theme, guys. Really dig down deep into it. Emmy, let's just say you were trying to gain more control over what you eat here—"

I inhaled sharply. If Tina really found out about the food, a Staffie would start following me around at meals again. That simply couldn't happen.

"—I'm not saying that you are," Tina said in that reassuring voice. "But if you were, what would make you want to make better food choices at Heartland?"

I decided it couldn't hurt to play along a little bit. "Well for one thing, I would tailor the calories to the individual. For someone my size, it should only be around fifteen hundred, not the two or three thousand I'm expected to eat every day here." I doubled what I normally shot for because adults always seemed to want to shove way too much food down kids' throats.

"Again, hypothetically, what if I could arrange that? Would you feel less inclined to ask others to eat your food?"

I nodded. "Sure, I guess so. Hypothetically."

"Great!" Tina exclaimed. "Consider it done!"

I wasn't sure if she was for real or what, but if she was, I was golden. Reduced food meant I'd only need one person to clear the excess on my plate, not five. I didn't like asking for help or being in the hole any favors. Mohammed had told us a million times how back in Sierra Leone, they were always starving and he would probably never feel full because of that, so there would be no indebtedness when he was my only garbage disposal. He wanted my food and I wanted it gone. It would be a mutual favor.

"Now let's move on to escape plans," Tina said, focusing her attention on Diana. "What would make a student dislike Heartland so much that they'd try to run away and put their lives at risk, not to mention the level they've achieved here?"

This was such a silly question, we all had to laugh. There were a million and one reasons to hate Assland.

"No Wi-Fi on our computers!" Justin called out. Chip high-fived him, and it was official: My crush on Justin, which had been hanging on by a thread since he'd turned kind of surly, was officially over. I'd had it up to here with guys who only cared about naked pictures of girls but not the girls in the pictures.

"No hookups allowed!" Chip shouted.

"No family here," Mohammed piped in.

"Not enough bacon and pork chops!" Diana said, cackling and oinking away, leaving Jenny looking more pained than usual.

"Nothing to do," I added quietly. "Nothing fun, I mean." The most fun thing I'd done since I got here was go off campus to 7-Eleven with Brittany to celebrate my being up for level two. The change hadn't been approved yet because my Contemporary American Family teacher said I hadn't been sharing enough. I had until the end of next week to show I trusted everyone enough to participate more in class. If I did, I'd be moving up, and the best thing about that would be getting to talk to Joss.

As promised, she'd e-mailed me little dispatches from home

every day, keeping me in the loop about all the gossip at school. I wrote her back old-fashioned letters almost as regularly, which the staff then scanned into the office computer and e-mailed back to her. Joss obviously wasn't getting any of the dirt about Assland since what I wrote was reviewed for inappropriate content. I couldn't wait to tell her the real scoop.

"The rules around Internet access and relationships aren't something I have control over," Tina said. "But family, food, and fun? I might be able to do something about those. Let's get even more specific, okay?"

"I need to be able to talk to my family more often," Mohammed said. "Make sure the ones I have left aren't getting killed or anything."

Tina nodded. "Well, we have Family Weekend coming up at the end of the month, where you'll all get to spend quality time with your loved ones. And though I really doubt your family has been killed"—she nodded at Mohammed—"I'll talk to your individual therapist about having more contact with your mom and dad until then. How's that?"

Mohammed didn't look happy at about it all. In fact, he looked like he was about to go postal.

Justin was squinting at Mohammed. "Dude, I thought you said you watched your dad die when you were four!"

Mohammed roared back. "Don't you ever mention my father again!"

"You mean the fake dead one or the real alive one?" Chip asked calmly.

"Boys!" Tina yelled, standing up. "Let's get back to the subject at hand. Can you think of a wholesome activity you'd like to do together as a group?"

We all sat there and stared at our fingernails, our feet, the wall. Wholesome was not what any of us wanted. It was Diana who finally broke the silence.

"I want to go here," she said, shoving the crumpled-up state fair brochure at Tina. It was covered with pictures of cows and funnel cakes and Ferris wheels.

Tina read it and smiled. "I think we can make this happen. I'll even chaperone. If everyone stays off academic probation and has no angry outbursts this week, that is. So let's say Friday, shall we?"

"Yesssssss!" Diana said.

"This was quite a group today, kids," Tina said, nodding at each of us. "I'll keep my part of the deal if you keep yours. Work together as a team, okay? I'm really looking forward to our field trip."

"Me too," Diana agreed.

"Why you so hopped up about a cheesy fair anyhow, Diana?" Chip asked.

"Because Joey Chestnut is gonna be there!" she said.

I had no clue who he was. "Who?"

"Joey Chestnut! The hot dog eating champ!" she explained.

"Why in hell would you care about him?" Justin wanted to know.

"Because he's hot. And because if I can't get any in here, at least I can eat a ton of wieners at the fair. Like, get really porked, you know?"

Diana kept laughing until Jenny handed her a note. Diana read it out loud: "'It's okay to use some variation of the word pig as sexual innuendo. Pigs are very passionate, you know.'"

CHAPTER 12

JUSTIN

SO IT HAD COME TO THIS. I WAS ON MY BEST BEHAVIOR SO I COULD go to a fair. Carnies, fried food, and livestock. Oh yeah, and a hot dog eating contest. Awesome.

The worst part was that I was actually kind of excited about it. Which I recognized made it the first thing I'd been excited about in a long time. Which meant that as a therapeutic technique, it was kind of working. Which pissed me off.

Not that I was happy or anything. It was more like I was walking around and everything was gray, and the idea of the stupid fair was the one spot of color.

"So what conclusions can you draw from this?" Max asked me in my one-on-one.

"I guess that if you bore the crap out of people for long enough, then anything, no matter how crappy, will seem like a relief."

Max smiled. "You are a stubborn kid, you know that?"

"I have been told this in the past, yes. But why do you say that now?"

"Because you are so determined to be pissed off that you can't even enjoy a victory. You were in a bad place, a really low place, and you might not be out of it yet, but it has gotten marginally better. And you can't even enjoy it or even admit that it happened. You think it's a trick, but it's not. I mean, this is pretty much what we have to offer people with your diagnosis. Not that you're never going to have low patches, but just that you can hang on to the knowledge that they won't last forever. Isn't that good?"

I thought about this for a minute. "I guess. I don't know. I think it would be better if I never had to feel so awful."

"And it would be better if I didn't have to test my blood every day and inject insulin," Max said. "Type one diabetes. But that's not the hand I got dealt. I got the hand with a lot of needles in it. And you got the depressive hand."

"Well, this hand sucks."

"No question. But nobody's life is perfect. Why do you think it's so hard for you to accept the imperfections in yours?"

I thought about this for a minute. "Because," I said. Not much of an answer, but it was all I had.

Max tapped his iPad. "Here's what we're gonna do," he said. "We're gonna do some work figuring out your core issue."

"Awesome," I said in a flat voice. "What's that?"

"It's a deep-seated belief you have that is messing up how you see the world."

"Great. Something else to look forward to," I said.

The prospect of digging into my deep-seated beliefs made the idea of having one night of relief at the fair that much more enticing. I was just about beside myself with excitement about an event I would have mocked mercilessly six months ago. Okay, six days ago.

And though I really wanted the fair, I wanted it less than Diana. Who had just decided she was the general of our little army of freaks. So Tuesday at dinner, I got this from her:

"Justin. History test tomorrow. Have you studied?"

"Have you heard of anhedonia?" I shot back.

"Is that a vocabulary word for your history test?"

"No, it's something that those of us with depression experience, and it's—"

"If it's not on the test, I don't give a shit right now. You need to get a C to stay off probation, and—Emmy. Nobody buys that 'spit the chewed food into the napkin while pretending to wipe your mouth' gag. Cut it out. Just eat. You're a freaking skeleton already, and I'm pretty sure if you blow away in one of these high prairie winds, I'm not gonna get to see Joey Chestnut. So eat up."

Mohammed gave a heavy sigh.

"You got something to say, Sri Lanka?"

Mohammed put down his fork. "Sierra Leone, idiot."

"Whatever. I'm never going to either place."

Mohammed gave Diana a serious look. The kind that, for a guy, would have a serious beating at the end of it. "I just . . . you know. The whole idea of an *eating* contest. It's obscene. In my country there are people *starving*, and here you've got so much abundance—"

"I know, right?" Diana said. "Like you, for example, have an extra parent we've never heard about before! So wasteful!"

"I—" Mohammed began.

"He's right, though," Emmy chimed in as she sawed a cherry tomato into eight identical pieces. "Look at all the obesity in our country."

Mohammed nodded. "Right. And you've got so much that you're willing to make *a game* out of it, and I'm supposed to behave so you can go watch this obscene spectacle that, frankly, makes me sick."

Chip put his burger down. "That is *it*! That is just it. Shut the hell up, Tracy."

Everybody looked at Chip like he was insane. Well, I mean, more insane than we'd previously thought.

And I guess I should say, everybody but me looked at Chip that way. I shot him a look that attempted to communicate this: "Shut up. We agreed we were going to save this ill-gotten information for a time when it was really necessary, and I'm pretty sure it's not necessary right now, and by the way I have to share a room with this dude."

"Who's Tracy?" Diana asked.

Chip put on a sports announcer voice and gestured at Mohammed. "Tracy Jefferson, ladies and gentlemen! Hailing from Grosse Pointe, Michigan, he's the son of two physicians, and until recently attended prestigious Milton Academy in Milton, Massachusetts, the alma mater of former US Senators Robert and Ted Kennedy!"

There was a moment of silence. Everyone just stared at Mohammed/Tracy, who was doing his deep breathing, trying-not-to-snap thing. And then Diana started to laugh. It began as these kinds of snorts coming out of her nose, and then it erupted into what I can only describe as guffaws.

"Tracy! I was scared of a . . . a boy named Tracy!"

Emmy snorted, too, and this set me off. Pretty soon everybody was laughing, and even though I was looking at Mohammed—sorry, Tracy—and seeing that he was about to do something that was totally going to wreck our chances of going to the fair and I really should have stopped and tried to hustle him away from the table, I couldn't move. I was laughing too hard. And it felt great. I couldn't remember the last time I laughed until my stomach hurt, and right then it was killing me.

And then Tracy's rage face suddenly broke, and he was

laughing, too. "Man, I got you bitches good!" he said between laughs. "The civil war in Sierra Leone ended . . . in 2002."

This caused another round of hysterical laughter, and when Tracy came up for air he said, "So easy to scare you bitches . . . my mom wouldn't let me try out for lacrosse because it's . . . too violent! You racist assholes are scared of anybody black!"

I was now actually crying from laughing so hard. I mean, yeah, I'd known that my supposedly African roommate was actually a rich kid from Michigan since Chip hacked into the school records on his netbook, but still, knowing that scary, rage-filled Mohammed from Sierra Leone was actually a mama's boy who wasn't allowed to play lacrosse and who'd just been messing with us for weeks was just really funny. I mean, he got us. He totally got us.

"So," I said. "How long has this been going on?"

"Just since this group started. I was Didier Mogumba, soccer prodigy from Paris, in the group I was in before this."

Diana wiped tears away from her eyes and extended a hand across the table. "Well played, my friend. Well played," she said, and Tracy shook her hand.

Later, as we were lying in the rule-mandated darkness of our room at 10:30 p.m., I asked Tracy, "So, were you just, like, sick of being you? Is that what the whole thing was about?" Because that was kind of appealing to me—the idea that you could just throw off your entire screwed-up self and substitute somebody else with different problems. And if you were as good at it as Tracy is, that person would actually become kind of real. I mean, if you convinced five people that someone existed, doesn't that make them kind of real?

There was a long silence that made me wonder if Tracy was asleep. "Naaah," he said. "I just like fucking with people. I mean, really, I don't hate being Tracy Jefferson. I just like being Tracy Jefferson who gets people to believe a bunch of stupid crap more."

"So who's the girl? I mean, the one you talk to when you're supposedly talking to your mom? The one you were all uptight to get extra time on the phone with?"

"Which one?" he said, and laughed. "I mean, that's why I always need extra time on the phone, you know?"

I laughed, though, of course, I didn't know. But I could imagine.

"Who do these girls think they're talking to?"

"Let's see. Latasja thinks she's talking to Rakim, Elizabeth thinks she's talking to Shane, and Tracy thinks she's talking to C-Dogg."

"Tracy? Like, really, you're dating a girl with your same name?"

"No. C-Dogg is dating a girl with my same name. It's a weird world, Justin."

Well, that was certainly true. I lay in silence for a minute or two before asking one more question.

"One g or two?"

"What?"

"C-Dogg. One g or two?"

"Two, of course. Don't wake me up to ask me stupid questions."

Okay, then.

The next morning at breakfast, everybody—except Jenny, of course—made a big show of saying "Good morning . . . Tracy," and smiling.

We were about halfway through breakfast when Tracy turned to Chip, who was sitting next to him, and said, "Okay, Chip. As far as I can tell, we now know everybody's real name except yours—"

"It's Chip!"

"Bullshit," Tracy said, "Nobody puts Chip on a birth certificate. I'm from Grosse Pointe, remember? I know me some Chips. And nobody named Chip is really named Chip."

"Okay, okay. It's—"

"Wait. I'm not done. We're all pretty clear on why everybody else is here—Skeletor over there is kind of obvious, and so's Mopey"—he gestured at me with his fork—"Psycho"—that's Diana—"Silent"—Jenny—"and"—he pointed a thumb at his chest—"the compulsive liar. And then there's Chip."

"Chesterton," Chip said.

"*Chesterton?*" Diana asks. "As in The Molesterton?"

"That doesn't make any sense," Chip said. "And yeah, that's

the name on my birth certificate. It's a family name. And if you don't mind, I'd really rather go by Chip."

"Whatever, Chesterton," Diana said.

"And it's a crack addiction." Everybody stared. "World of Warcrack, that is," Chip said, and smiled.

"Wait," Tracy said. "They locked you up for a video game addiction?"

"They locked you up for lying?" Chip shot back.

Tracy took a breath. "Well. I may have, um . . . run a bit of a grift on my fellow students at Milton Academy. There may have been five figures of restitution my parents had to make. But we're not talking about me. We're talking about you."

"I wanna hear about the grift!" Diana yelled.

"Long con. Basically a Ponzi scheme. I got a bunch of classmates to invest in my nonexistent drug business. Front me cash to make a buy, I'll move the product, and double your money. But there's no product and no buy. Just more suckers putting up money for drugs I never bought."

We all stared at him for a minute.

"You, sir, are an artist," I said.

"Unless he's lying now about lying then," Diana said.

"Whatever," Tracy harrumphed. "Can we get back to Chip's video game addiction?"

"I used to play for days. Days. I bought diapers so I wouldn't have to get out of my chair to pee, okay?"

"Really? I mean, really, or is this like a Tracy thing where you're making up something outrageous and seeing how much you can get us to believe?" I asked.

"Swear to God."

"What's it like? Peeing in a diaper, I mean."

"Warm. At first. It gets clammy later. Poo, of course, is much worse."

And that pretty much did it for everyone's appetite. Everyone, strangely, but Emmy, who continued her normal food dissection. Everybody stared at her. "What?" she said.

Finally, it was Friday afternoon. Classes? Over. Homework? Done. Dinner? Eaten. Chores? Everything was clean as a freaking whistle. Finally, we were allowed to leave. It turned out that Assland had one of those extra-long vans that seated about fifteen people. The staff guy who wasn't Tiny (or tiny) was on driving duty. He said something like, "Don't know how I got talked into this one," and shut the plastic window that separated the driver's seat from the rest of us.

"Alright! Who's ready for the fair!" Tina chirped as she ushered us into our seats.

"Yyyyyyyeahhhhhh!" Diana screamed, and everybody else just kind of looked at her.

I found myself next to Emmy. "You know, if you time it just right, you can eat a ton of food and then puke it up from the rides," I offered.

Something was different about the way she looked at me. "If

you time it right, you can throw yourself out of a roller coaster car and kill yourself," she replied.

"Yeah, you have to be pretty seriously suicidal to throw yourself off a high carnival ride," I said. "I'm more of a 'cry for help' kind of guy."

"Right, I forgot," Emmy said. Her smile faded almost instantly, and she stared out the window at the endless rows of corn and soybeans.

After a while, I got the hint she wasn't in a talking mood—at least to me—so I closed my eyes and fell asleep.

13.

EMMY

THE RIDE TO THE FAIR WAS LONG, FLAT, AND BORING. JUSTIN HAD gotten on the van and made some mean joke about my eating habits again, which only confirmed what I'd already decided: He was no longer flirt-worthy. And now that he was snoring away next to me—what was he, a toddler who nodded off every time he was in a moving vehicle?—it only made me more sure of my lack of feelings for him.

With Justin snoozing, Diana deep into conversation with Tina about Joey Chestnut's hot dog eating strategies, and Chip and Tracy playing poker in the last seat of the van, I had plenty of time to think. I set my mind on figuring out what I was going to say in my Contemporary American Family class to get my level change approved.

So far, we'd tackled single-parent households, same-sex parenting, the foster care system, and being raised by extended family members. After each topic, the teacher always asked for people who had grown up in that situation to share their thoughts on the benefits and drawbacks of the arrangement as they had experienced it.

The kids with single parents said they appreciated how close they were with the parent they lived with, but were mad at the other parent for leaving. The ones with the same-sex parents thought it was a cool way to grow up, but hated how homophobes thought their moms or dads should burn in hell for loving each other. The foster kids liked being part of a family rather than living in a group home but complained about a lack of consistency. The ones living with extended family loved Gram and Gramps or Auntie and Uncle but missed their parents. Next week we were set to talk about adoptive families, so I would definitely be expected to add something major to the discussion. And whatever I said needed to be honest, or no level change and no talking to Joss for who knew how much longer. I couldn't just bullshit my way through it.

But what was there to say, really? My mom and dad were still together, they were generally cool as far as parents went, no one wanted them to go to hell, and I'd been given support and consistency from the day I'd been adopted. I basically had your run-of-the-mill normal life—no big controversies or traumas—with the added wrinkle that I was the only one in the family who didn't come from the same DNA. I couldn't figure out a good way to tell the class how crappy it felt to be the outsider in your own family—even a nice, normal, nonabusive family—without sounding like a whiny little bitch.

I decided writing down some ideas might help me with that one, so I got up and went over to where Jenny was sitting. Her journal was like her best friend, and when other people were busy having conversations, she'd usually just write away in it. I figured the odds were good she'd have it with her even on a van ride to a state fair. But when I asked to borrow a pen and paper, she patted the seat next to her instead.

"If you're going to tell me to f-off and punch me in the stomach again, I'd rather not," I told her.

She shook her head and smiled, pointing to the spot again.

"What's up?" I said, sitting down. I wasn't expecting anything in response, of course.

She sat and stared at her hands for a solid minute. Then she sighed, took a deep breath, and whispered, "What is it with you two?"

My eyes flew open and I looked around to see if anyone else had witnessed this momentous occasion—Jenny had actually talked! But everyone was still deep into whatever else it was they were doing.

"Who two?" I asked once I'd gotten over my shock.

"You and Justin," she said softly.

I cocked my head to the side and scrunched up my nose. "Nothing. Why?"

She shrugged. "Sometimes, I thought you liked him but he missed all the cues. Other times, it seemed like he liked you but you'd just blow him off. Like when he got on the van today. So I guess I'm just trying to figure out if there's anything there, or if it's my imagination."

"All in your head. He definitely doesn't like me," I assured her. "Mostly, our conversation consists of him busting my chops about the way I eat. And I don't know . . . maybe Women and the Media class is getting to me, but I don't like how he objectifies and commodifies women by watching porn. So I guess that means I don't like him either."

Jenny patted my knee. "If you rule out all the guys who like porn as potential dates, I think you're going to be alone a lot."

I laughed. "That's okay. I was already on a planned hiatus from guys until college."

"That must have been one hell of a breakup," she said.

"It would have been," I admitted. "If we were ever official in the first place. Which we weren't."

"Care to share?" she asked.

"And admit how stupid I was? Um, probably not."

I hadn't told anyone except Joss—not my friends, parents, school administrators, Brittany, no one—the real deal about what had gone down. I'd sworn Joss to secrecy for life, and she'd promised to go to her grave with my dirt. So I couldn't imagine telling Jenny the whole sordid tale now, not after the lengths I'd gone to cover up my shame.

Too bad that didn't stop me from reliving the nightmare unrelationship in my mind. It had all started back in September, when I was assigned Mason as my lab partner in chemistry. Mason was basically king of the school, and not someone who would have even known I existed if it hadn't been for the alphabetical proximity of our last names.

As with most kings, Mason had a queen, and they'd been going out forever—like at least two years. Mason and Lizbeth were destined for all the cutesy senior superlatives: Most Popular, Best Couple, Most Likely to Get Married and Live Happily Ever After With Two Gorgeous Kids and a Golden Retriever, the works. So when Mason asked me to study with him for our first test, I might have been a little intimidated to be hanging out with such a cool senior, but I definitely knew it wasn't code for "let's fool around."

We both aced that exam, which was enough to convince us both that studying together was a smart strategy. And after maybe our third session, the strictly business thing started morphing into something else. I would never have imagined a guy like Mason and I have anything in common, but it turned out there was plenty. We both liked horror flicks, pugs, Harry Potter, and Sudoku. We were obsessed with Scrabble, jalapeño-pineapple pizza, and the smell of vanilla extract. Our siblings were our best friends. By then, I'd almost say we were becoming more than study buddies, albeit buddies who only saw each other in chem class and every so often when we were hitting the books together at my house or his.

And then one night, when we were cramming for our midterm, Mason wasn't acting like his usual laid-back self. Naturally I asked him what was up.

"I broke up with Lizbeth today," he said, with a half happy, half sad look on his face. "And she kind of freaked out on me. It was not pretty."

I felt my heart skip a happy little dance inside my chest, though I tried my best to keep that under wraps. "Well, you guys were together for like, forever, so of course she's upset. But I'm sure she'll get over it," I said, adding quickly. "I mean, not that you'd be easy to get over or anything."

The minute that last part left my mouth, I wanted to suck the words right back into my lungs. I knew it sounded like I had a crush on Mason, and of course by that time I did. A whopper.

But I shouldn't have worried. He'd broken into a huge grin. "I was kind of hoping you'd say that, because there's someone else I like . . ."

He trailed off and went in for a kiss. It was *killer*. One of the best moments in my entire life, even now that I knew how shitty it had all ended up. Fireworks went off in every molecule of my body. Parts of me I didn't even know existed tingled.

We made out the rest of the supposed study session and for the first time, got Bs on our tests. I didn't care in the least. My grade for the semester was still an A, and now I had this great guy to go along with my awesome GPA.

Except I didn't really *have* him. At least, not as far as anyone else knew. He'd asked that we keep our "thing"—whatever it was—on the down low because he didn't want to hurt Lizbeth's feelings by dumping her and asking me out all in the same day. This indicated to me that Mason was a nice, compassionate person, so I was all too happy to comply. I figured things would work themselves out soon enough.

After a couple of months, though, Lizbeth still hadn't rebounded. If anything, she was worse than ever. She was kind of disappearing before everyone's eyes. Her clothes started hanging off her body, she looked gaunt, her eyes were hollow. She wasn't the golden girl who had been Mason's girlfriend anymore. She'd gone from beautiful to brittle, from someone to be envied to someone to be pitied. Honestly, it was scary.

"Emmy, we'll let everybody know about us as soon as Lizbeth gets her shit together," he told me. "I promise. I just don't think it's fair to kick her when she's down though, you know?"

Again, I was totally on board. I mean, only the world's most heartless bitch would have rubbed how much Mason and I liked each other in a sick girl's face. And I wasn't that kind of girl.

But I didn't actually know what kind of girl I was anymore either, because I definitely wasn't acting like my normal self. As our relationship went further underground, our "study sessions" (which were now more like sexy sessions) and bathroom breaks at school (which were just excuses to make out anytime, anyplace we could, from the janitor's closet to the handicapped bathroom) got hotter and heavier than ever. There was something incredibly exciting about all the hiding and scheming and plotting and planning. It turned absolutely everything in me on, my brain and my body. I should have known I was in trouble, but the whole situation was just so intoxicating I kept going back for more.

And so one night when we were talking before bed like we always did and Mason asked me for a sexy pic, I was totally game.

"Only if you send me one, too," I'd told him, teasing the fun out to the maximum degree.

Five minutes later, I had one of him in my phone and he had one of me in his. I'd gone into the bathroom, locked the door, took off my shirt, made sure my B-cups were nicely pushed together, and snapped a few dozen topless (from the chin down so only he would know it was me, of course) pics. I picked the hottest one and sent it. He texted me hearts, I texted him a little devil emoticon and a smiley, and we signed off for the night.

I didn't think much more about it, no less regret it, until I stepped foot in the cafeteria the next day. Apparently when

Mason had gone to buy lunch, his friend Danny Schwartz decided to flip through all the pics on Mason's phone. And that's when he stumbled on my boob shot.

Everything might have been okay—I mean, my face wasn't in the shot, I'm not that stupid—but it seemed I'd made a huge tactical error. In my bathroom, my mom had just put up those decorative tin letters they have at Urban Outfitters. Which meant reflected in the mirror of my edgy nude shot was Y-M-M-E. I'd just been outed.

Danny started in on the "me so horny" thing immediately, often adding with a big fat guffaw that he thought my nipples would've been slanted instead of round. What's worse, he started a rumor that I was the reason Lizbeth had gone off the deep end—that I'd been so obsessed with Mason I'd barraged him with nude pictures until he'd broken down and started having sex with me, which Lizbeth then found out about. It was total bullshit, but everyone bought it.

By the end of the day, the entire school thought I was a total slut. I'd gone from nobody knowing or caring who I was to everyone hating me. It might have been bearable if Mason had taken a big stand in my defense, but as far as I could tell he maybe weakly protested the theory the first day and then said pretty much nothing after that.

Bad enough, that still wasn't rock bottom. The next week, he and Lizbeth got back together. *You know I still love you, right?*

he'd texted me after they went public. *But I can't be responsible for her being so sick anymore, you know? It makes me feel terrible.*

What he failed to recognize was what a terrible situation all this left me in. I mean, why wouldn't people believe I'd been this weird stalker? Mason had never so much as taken me out for a Starbucks. My friends—everyone except Joss—started avoiding me like everyone else in school.

"I seriously don't believe you did that when you saw how it affected Lizbeth!" one even came right out and said to me.

I protested, asserted my innocence, stood up for myself—and it did absolutely nothing in the end. No one wanted to take the pariah girl's side. It made me alternately furious and depressed times a thousand. I finally decided revenge was the only way I'd ever get any satisfaction. For Danny, I chose the online attack strategy. For Mason, I chose the same weapon as his girfriend had: Noticeable weight loss. That would teach those mother-fuckers to ruin my life.

"Come on, I'd love to hear about the bad relationship that wasn't. I'm talking to you, right? And that's hard for me," Jenny said.

I looked up and saw Tina giving Jenny the thumbs-up. She tried to pretend she had just been running her fingers through her hair when I noticed. Tina wasn't the most subtle when it came to breakthroughs.

"Why *are* you talking to me now?" I asked, trying to steer the subject away from the whole Mason debacle and ridiculous Justin question. "I mean, not that I don't like it. I do. It's just that you had so many opportunities when we're in our room and it's just been dead silence. It would've been nice to have someone to talk to before now."

"My goal is to head home after the next Family Weekend. That gives me just about a month to get to level six. I've been stuck on four forever because I haven't let someone new into my 'speaking circle'"—here she put her fingers up in air quotes—"as the Asslandians like to call it. I have to show I can be 'proactive' and 'empowered,' you know."

I gave a little laugh. "Asslandians! Good one!" I said. "I hope you make it."

Tina turned around, all smiles. "I have a feeling she will, especially after that big step!"

Jenny beamed, but I felt shittier than ever.

CHAPTER 14

JUSTIN

I WOKE UP WHEN THE VAN STOPPED. "STATE FAIRGROUNDS, everybody!" Tina called out, and everybody kind of started moving in slow motion. Everybody except Diana, that is.

"Okay, who's too chickenshit to go on the puke rides? 'Cause I wanna ride everything, and if you guys are too weak to take it, I'm gonna have to sit next to some black-toothed meth-addicted local yokel, and that does not make me happy because they might try to kidnap me because I'm pretty."

"Not to mention good-natured," Chip said, and everybody except Diana laughed.

Diana shot back, "Listen, Frodo. Keep talking and I will put my foot so far up your ass that my toenails will be your teeth."

At this, Tina blew an airhorn. The sound was excruciating as it bounced around the metal box we were in, and everybody froze and looked at Tina.

"Okay, listen up, guys. I need you to understand something. As you may have gathered, this little trip is not standard procedure at Assland."

There was stunned silence. Finally Diana said, "You . . . you called it . . ."

"I know what I called it, Diana," Tina said, smiling. "This is in order to emphasize something. We are not on campus. It's impossible for anybody to monitor what happens here. And I want you to know very well that I understand the temptation to misbehave. That's why I just did it."

"Ooo, you said ass," Tracy said. "Big deal."

Tina stared at him. "Shit. Fuck. Queef. Happy?"

Emmy snorted. "Did you really just say—"

"Yes. Now listen. I've really gone out on a limb for you guys. Okay? I begged, wheedled, and cajoled the administration into allowing you guys to have some extra privileges, because I really believe that the teamwork you've been showing in the past few weeks is a great thing and is really helping all of you. I spent an hour on the phone with each one of your parents getting their approval for this."

I, for one, was impressed. "Did you actually talk to my dad for an hour?" I wasn't sure anyone had gotten an hour of his time in the last sixteen years.

Tina looked at me. "I did. He's very worried about you."

I didn't want to be thinking about that asshole on a night when I was supposed to be having fun, so I didn't go any further with this conversation.

"All I'm saying is this: I have put my own ass on the line for you. And if you screw this up by doing anything even remotely unethical or illegal, then I am most likely finished at this school. Don't make me look like an idiot for putting myself on the line for you. Okay?"

Everybody nodded, some of us kind of sheepishly.

"I didn't hear you. I said, Okay?"

"Okay, okay!" everybody said.

"Great. One more thing. Have fun tonight. You guys really have worked hard, and I'm really proud of you." Tina opened the doors of the van and we all filed out into the parking lot. I took a deep breath.

"Hmm . . . manure, car exhaust, fried food, and, unless I miss my guess, just a hint of BO," I said.

"It smells like freedom!" Diana yelled.

At the ticket booth, Tina bought us all plastic wristbands that meant we were good to go for all the rides. She also handed each of us a twenty dollar bill that she informed us all of our parents personally authorized. She furthermore told us we needed to be back at this exact spot three hours from now, and should we fail to appear by three hours and ten minutes from now, she had the state police on speed dial and we would be reported as runaways.

"So," I said to Chip and Tracy, "what are we gonna go on first?"

"You guys can go on whatever the hell you want," Tracy said. "I'm going to find some girls."

"And who are you tonight?" I asked.

"I think I'm Hakeem," Tracy said. "From the ATL, y'all. I'm tryin' out for the hoops team at state. Gotta get my scholarship on, yo. Make that paper, son."

"Parrot them cliché's, dawg," Emmy said. "Maybe it's not everybody else who's racist."

"What the hell do you mean?" Tracy said.

"Maybe you live in an all-white neighborhood and you do this crap because you hate how different you feel."

"Or maybe that's you," Tracy said.

Emmy smiled. "Oh, it's definitely me," she said. "But I think it might be you, too."

"I think he's just chickenshit," Diana said.

"I am not afraid to go on some carnival ride!" Tracy spat back.

"Really?" I said. "Because I kind of am. I mean, I don't have a whole lot of faith in the maintenance of these things—"

"He's afraid to be himself," Diana said.

"Why the hell would I be afraid to be myself?" Tracy asked.

"That's between you and your therapist," Diana said. "But when you move up a level by identifying that as your core issue, you can thank me. Now are you bitches going to go on some rides or what?"

Tilt-A-Whirl. Check. Cheesy, completely unscary haunted house. Check. Seats on a big pole that climbed the outside of the pole and then dropped down very quickly. Check. For an extra ten bucks, you could ride the Space Shot, which was a small metal cage attached to two springy cords attached to two giant cranes that shot you like seven hundred feet into the air. I was definitely passing on that ride, but Tracy, who I suspect was still smarting from Diana's chickenshit remark, ponied up the ten bucks, and once he was on, Diana had to go with him.

We stood to the side and watched the video feed from inside the cage on a big screen. It was hilarious—Diana laughed hysterically the whole time, while Tracy screamed with a look of pure terror on his face as the cage shot into the air and then bounced on the bungees, up and down for about a minute.

Of course we all—well, all of us but Jenny, who was not speaking and who had smiled but hadn't let out a single "whoo" on any ride—teased Tracy when he staggered off the ride. "Dude," Chip said between guffaws, "your face . . . you should have seen it. Oh my God I am totally buying the DVD just so I can watch you scream like a little girl—no, sorry, the little girl wasn't screaming like that . . ."

Tracy actually smiled. "Why don't you put some money down and go on it yourself and we'll see *your* face. At least I went on it. I tried something that was tough for me. All you guys did was stand and watch. And at least I'm not puking into a garbage can." He gestured at Diana, who was hunched over a fifty-five-gallon drum, barfing out the contents of her stomach.

The noises were horrifying, and I started feeling kind of nauseated myself. And then Diana stood up, wiped her mouth with the back of her arm, and said, "Okay. What's next?"

"How about the Ferris wheel?" Emmy said. "It's a little more . . . gentle."

We ambled over to the Ferris wheel. We stood in the line like everything was normal. And everything was normal for everyone else, but for me, it was definitely not. My heart was pounding so hard I thought it might actually pop out of my chest, and this was making it kind of hard for me to catch my breath. It was a cool night but I could feel the sweat popping out on my forehead. "Hey Justin," I heard Emmy's voice say. "You okay?"

"I . . . I don't think I can do this," I said. "I'm . . . I'm totally freaking out."

"Why?" Emmy said.

"I . . ." deep breath, "I . . . well, it's funny because it's not like a thrill ride or anything, but this one scares me more than any other ride. Like on the other ones you're totally strapped in and it's fine, but this is . . ."

"Are you afraid you're gonna fall out?" she asked.

"No," I said. "I'm afraid I'm gonna *jump* out."

She looked at me for a long time. "Well. Do you *want* to?"

"Not at all. That's why I'm scared. I guess it doesn't make a lot of sense, but that's mental illness for you," I said. "I mean, okay, like, yeah, go ahead and point and laugh because I'm pretty screwed up and I should be here. Not at the fair but Assland, I mean. It's like"—somehow I'd started to cry here—"this is something a normal kid should be able to do. Those are not thoughts a normal kid should have. I'm just . . . I'm fucking broken."

Emmy put her hand on my back. It felt really nice. I realized that apart from the odd punch to or from Tracy or Chip, I hadn't touched anybody or been touched by anybody in weeks.

"I'll sit next to you, and if it looks like you're gonna jump, I'll punch you in the 'nads really hard," she said. "Deal?"

"I'm just gonna sit this one out," I said.

"And live with everybody mocking you about it?" she asked.

"The key word in that sentence is 'live,'" I said.

Emmy looked at me for a minute. "What if you go up there and don't jump? And you don't even try to jump? What then?"

"I don't know. What would happen if you ate something here? Something disgustingly fatty?"

Emmy paused at this. "I don't know either. But I will if you will."

"You will what?"

"You go on the Ferris wheel and I will buy state fair food and eat it."

"You're gonna chicken out," I said.

"So are you," she said.

"The hell I am," I said, and so, with lots of deep breaths, I stood in the line next to Emmy, showed my wristband to the skinny guy with the acne-scarred face and the scraggly beard who ran the ride, and climbed into this easily–escaped–from bench, and sat there as we went spinning into the air.

I could feel Emmy watching me even though I had my eyes closed. On about the third spin around, I opened them up and saw the whole state fair below us. It was an awesome sight—lots of tiny people milling around in the yellow, red, and purple glow from the lights on the rides and the fried food stands. "It's kinda pretty, in its own gross way," I said.

"Yeah," Emmy said. "It's beautiful."

"I haven't jumped," I said.

"I noticed," she said. "I'm a little disappointed I haven't had the opportunity to punch you in the 'nads."

"Well, we're not off the ride yet," I said.

Emmy smiled—the first real smile I'd seen from her in days, maybe even weeks—and we made two more circuits, and I was just starting to feel kind of okay when the ride stopped with us at the very top. I clenched my eyes shut and gritted my teeth and tried to concentrate on taking deep breaths, but it wasn't easy.

"You okay now?" Emmy said.

"Listen," I said, "I don't want you to punch me in the 'nads, but if I could just hold your hand, totally not in a sleazy way or anything, but just because I need . . ."

She slipped her hand into mine, and I squeezed it really hard. The bench swung back and forth, and my eyes stayed shut. I blew a deep breath out of my lips. "Thanks," I said.

"Thanks for not being sleazy," she said, and I smiled, but I didn't let go of her hand, the one that was anchoring me to the world that existed outside of my head.

And the Ferris wheel moved a little, then stopped again. And again. And again. When we were at a height where jumping out would only cause nonlethal injuries, I let Emmy's hand go.

The scary carny lifted the bar on our seat and we went running down the ramp to where everyone else was waiting.

"Who's hungry?" Diana said, and I cast a look over at Emmy. She gave me a little nod.

"Um. Me," she said.

15.

EMMY

"SO WHAT'S ON THE MENU FOR THE SKELETON?" DIANA CACKLED as we walked toward the food trucks.

"Um, I'm right here," I told her. "I can hear you."

"I guess I couldn't see you when you were turned sideways," she said, laughing even harder. "You kind of disappear that way, you know?"

I stuffed a bunch of wadded-up bills into Justin's hand. "I'll take one of those and a Diet Coke," I said, pointing to the nearest vendor. The food fumes were wafting around me so much I could practically *see* the salt, fat, and grease in the air. Everyone else was *oohing* and *aahing* over how great it smelled, and all I wanted to do was run away so I wasn't tempted to stuff my face and ruin all my hard work.

"No way, sister," Diana said, grabbing the roasted corn on the cob just as Justin was handing it to me. "You're not gonna get out of this one by eating a friggin' vegetable on a stick."

Shit. It was the only thing I'd seen that would keep me from packing on the pounds. "Seriously, it's the corn or nothing," I told her.

"Honestly, don't you see how stupid this skinny thing is? You have no tits or ass left. No guy is ever gonna think you're hot."

"She kinda has a point," Chip butted in.

Like I cared what he thought. I had tits and an ass when I was with Mason—with him but not really with him, or whatever the hell we'd been to each other—and look where it had gotten me. Having none was safer as far as I was concerned.

"Whatever," I said with a little shrug.

Justin leaned over and whispered so no one else could hear. "Don't listen to them. You're fine whatever way you want to look."

I spun around and looked at him closely to see if he was being mean again. He seemed pretty sincere. *Thanks*, I mouthed at him.

Somehow, something had changed with Justin. A switch had flipped. Things were back to how they'd been when we first got to Assland—nice, funny, a little flirty—but now there was something extra. Maybe it was that trust we were both supposed to be working on for level two. Maybe we'd figured that one out, at least with each other, up there on the Ferris wheel.

"Well then, what about your family?" Tracy piped in. "You're always bitching and moaning about how you don't fit in with them, but then you do everything you can to make yourself look even more different. Stupid, isn't it?"

"It's already so obvious it doesn't matter what I weigh," I told him.

"Fuck the bullshit, Emmy. It's time to throw down," Tracy said.

"Dude! You just quoted Frey! I mean Frey's tattoo! I love that guy!" Chip said.

The rest of us turned to Tracy and Chip like, *Huh*?

Tracy high-fived Chip. "That guy who wrote the memoir that really wasn't a memoir. He's kinda my hero," Tracy explained. "Like, he made even Oprah and the whole country believe his bullshit. And anyway, that's what he has tattooed on his arm. FTBSITTTD. *Fuck the bullshit, it's time to throw down.*"

I thought to myself, *Yeah, maybe he's right. Maybe it is time to try something new.* This revenge stuff was getting old. It hadn't made Mason come back to me, and it certainly hadn't changed Danny's life in any measurable way. He'd maybe been embarrassed for a week. As for me, I'd gotten kicked out of school; I kind of hated myself and was starving all the time; I'd messed up my relationship with my parents; and I was stuck at Assland for the foreseeable future.

"Fine," I said, a totally badass idea forming in my brain. "I'll totally go for it as long as everyone else promises to, too. Like Tracy? No lying today. No matter what anyone asks you, you tell the truth. And Chip? No games whatsoever while we're here. No playing little roulette wheels for prizes, no betting on what horse or pig is gonna win the blue ribbon, nothing. Jenny, you actually have to speak. Not just to me, but to everyone, in front of other people, so Tina knows we're not making it up. Like . . . do some karaoke. Or whatever, as long as it's words coming out of your mouth in a public forum. And Diana? For once, you have to do something nice for someone else. I don't even care what it is."

Diana planted her hands on her hips. "I'm waiting to hear what you're going to do that's so great before I decide."

I pointed over to one of the gross food trucks. "I'll eat that thing," I said.

"The Whopping Wiener?" Diana asked, a huge smile spreading across her face.

I nodded.

"If you're going to chow down on a foot-long hot dog topped with everything plus the garbage disposal, why not just enter the hot dog eating contest along with my dude Joey Chestnut?"

It was a completely ridiculous idea. Other than the few I was forced to gag down when I first got to Assland—before I cut the deal that got the guys eating my food on the daily—I hadn't eaten a full meal in ages, no less downed a zillion hot dogs in a few minutes. I was about to tell her no way when everyone else started chanting.

"Em-*my*! Em-*my*! Em-*my*! Em-*my*!"

"Fine." It kind of felt like I had friends again, and I kind of liked it—even if my friends here were total psychos and screwups. "You're on."

"I bet it'll be the first time you've ever had a wiener in your mouth," Diana said, waggling her eyebrows at me.

This sent me into another flashback of me and Mason. In my basement. In his bedroom. In the handicapped bathroom at school. Yeah, I'd experienced quite a bit of what Diana was referring to.

Diana started pealing out her maniacal laugh like usual, but stopped when she saw the stricken look on my face. "Wait . . . did some asshole make you do that? I'll frickin' kill the douche bag!"

"He didn't make me," I practically whispered.

"If you didn't really want to do it, then it's just as bad," Diana insisted, even though I'd been perfectly happy to do whatever Mason wanted to when we were together (or I guess, when I thought we were together but he was just using me). "What else did the douche lord make you do?"

I wasn't sure whether I was going to laugh or cry, so I ended up doing a little of both: Laughing *and* crying. "Send him a titty shot," I choked out.

Chip stared pointedly at my chest. "But . . . you don't . . ."

I crossed my arms across my noexistent boobs and let out much more of a laugh than a cry this time. "I used to, about twenty pounds ago."

Tracy threw an arm around me. "Truth? I never thought of you as, like, a sexual being before. But now I'm getting kind of horny picturing you twenty pounds ago, getting your freak on with that nasty white boy."

I chucked his arm off my shoulder and laughed some more. It felt good, and real, for the first time since Mason got rid of me like so much trash. "I think I'm gonna regret making you tell the whole truth and nothing but the truth for an entire day," I told him.

"Too late now," Tracy said with a wink. "So we're all in, right guys?"

Everyone agreed except Justin. "Wait, what about me?" he asked.

I smiled at him. "You already went balls out today on the Ferris wheel."

"I call bullshit!" Diana yelled. "We *all* went on that stupid Ferris wheel. It was a total baby ride."

"Yeah," I told her. "But Justin was the only one who thought he was going to jump out of it once we got to the top, and he still went on."

Diana considered this, then nodded. "Yeah, that's totally badass. Not killing yourself even when you think you want to. Takes a lot more balls to stay alive, don't you think?"

We all smiled because it was the truth: Living did take a lot more guts than giving up.

CHAPTER 16

JUSTIN

I HAD TO HAND IT TO HER. EMMY WENT UP TO THE BOOTH NEXT TO the stage like she did this every day and tried to enter the hot dog eating contest.

The woman seated in the booth looked like she had won a few eating contests of her own in her day, and she shook her head. "Darlin', this is the state fair. You don't just walk up and enter a contest with Joey Chestnut! Every farm boy with a big appetite for two hundred miles figures, well, if that kid can win, so can I. They started signing up right after the last one ended. And bless your heart, you're no bigger than a minute. Unless you've got a hollow leg, I don't see how you'd stand much of a chance against this field. Now how many tickets do y'all want?"

Emmy walked away looking dejected. "Well, I tried."

"The contest was a chickenshit move anyway," Jenny said.

We all walked on for about two steps before any of us realized that Jenny had just spoken.

"Wait wait wait," Tracy said. "You just talked!"

Chip went up for the high five, but Jenny left him hanging. "I mean. I thought this was, like, we were all trying our things, and you talked, so . . . "

Jenny looked at us like it was no big deal, and Emmy was in her face right away.

"Like hell it's a chickenshit move! You know what's a chickenshit move? Not talking for months at a time! That's what's chickenshit. Hiding from the world behind a wall of silence."

"I'd just like to jump in here and compliment my friend Emmy on the excellent metaphor," I said, and while neither she nor Jenny even seemed to notice that I said anything, Diana nodded in agreement.

"Entering an eating contest is a chickenshit move because everybody barfs in eating contests. It's kind of expected. It's part of the sick reason sick people watch them," Jenny clarified.

"Hey!" Diana yelled. "That's actually a big part of why I like 'em. Can't resist a good puke scene, you know?"

"So," Jenny continued, "that way you were gonna get to eat without having to worry about the food staying with you and giving you boobs somebody might actually want to see."

Emmy sputtered, and Jenny, seeing her opponent on the

ropes, went for the KO. "So the whole time you were giving us a pep talk, you were thinking about how you could weasel out of your thing."

Emmy looked kind of ashamed.

"Damn," I said. "That is some freaking brilliant manipulation! I would have thought only Tracy could have done that. My hat is off to you. Or it would be, if I had a hat."

"I didn't do it on purpose," Emmy said. "I mean, it wasn't really a conscious thing. And I'm not chickenshit. Diana. Order me a Whopping Wiener with everything."

Diana ran off, grinning, and returned with the Whopping Wiener.

After Diana's earlier "wiener in your mouth" remark, I felt kind of creepy gathering in a circle to watch Emmy eat a big one. But not actually creepy enough not to do it.

And any kind of perverted sexual thrill I might have gotten from the scene dissolved pretty much the instant Emmy took her first bite. The Whopping Wiener, which was smothered in, as near as I could tell, onions, mustard, relish, chili, Cheez Whiz or some similar cheese analogue, and hot sauce that Diana had added with a very heavy hand, was not something that could be eaten sexily. Or even neatly. Or really any way but disgustingly.

But I had to give it to her here, too—Emmy chowed it. Her face was soon a red and yellow mess of chili and Cheez Whiz, and she stopped only occasionally to belch as she did battle with the Whopping Wiener. It was a quick, if messy battle, and Emmy emerged from it looking stunned, semiconscious, and pleased with herself.

"Nap . . . kins," she said as a drip of chili-cheese ran off her chin and plopped to the dirt at her feet. Diana produced a stack and handed them to Emmy, who began slowly cleaning off her face.

"I'm not gonna lie," Tracy said. "That was straight-up disgusting. Any kind of horniness I might have had evaporated there."

Emmy looked at him and belched in response. "Oh my God. I missed food. I had no idea how much I missed food. That was horrible and gross and probably the best thing I ever ate. I don't think I've given bingeing a fair shot. Why bother purging one piece of cantaloupe when you can stuff your face and then get rid of it all, right?"

"Don't even *think* about purging now," Jenny said.

"Promise," Emmy said. "I'm gonna let this one run its course. And by the way, I think you're all gonna be suffering the consequences of that decision when you have to ride in a van with me later. I have no idea what my guts are going to do with chili, but I suspect it's not going to be pretty."

"Great," Jenny said. "Now I wanna show you guys something."

We followed Jenny through the state fairgrounds, and it was only when we almost got to the livestock barns—at least that was where I thought we were because the smell of hay and crap was thick in the air—that we realized Chip wasn't with us.

"Um. Hey Jenny. I hate to interrupt whatever point you're making here, but it looks like we lost one."

Everybody stopped and looked around. "Where the hell is Chip?" Emmy said.

"Does looking for his sorry ass count as doing something for someone else?" Diana asked.

"No," Emmy said.

"Damn."

"Well, we all know where we're gonna find him," Tracy said. "The midway."

We trudged back to the rows of rip-off carnival games. Sketchy guys in sleeveless T-shirts tried to mock us into throwing rings at ducks or shooting baskets at too-small hoops or throwing baseballs at bottles that were probably made of lead.

"I got him," Tracy said, pointing at the booth where a row of kids were shooting streams of water into the mouths of clowns.

"I never understood that," Diana said. "Like, you shoot water into the mouth of the clown and it makes a balloon fill with air and explode. What the hell sense does that make? I'd like it better if the clown's head exploded. I hate clowns."

Chip was surrounded by the following items: A medium-sized SpongeBob SquarePants, two large stuffed Dora the Explorers, and a colossal Perry the Platypus.

"Gimme that," Diana said, grabbing one of the Doras. "You don't need two." She tucked it under her arm and gave us all a look that dared us to make fun of her. I was sure as hell not going to be the one to do it.

Chip was too intent on watering his clown to pay much attention. So Tracy grabbed the squirt gun and turned it on Chip's face. "Ah! What the hell! I was gonna win that one!" Chip yelled.

"Guys, grab him," Emmy said, and so Tracy grabbed one arm and I grabbed another. Chip let us lead him away without much of a struggle. He actually looked kind of embarrassed and didn't protest at all as Jenny and Emmy distributed his winnings to actual children.

"Dammit! I could have totally done that! Why didn't you tell me?" Diana said when Emmy and Jenny rejoined us.

"Well, see, part of the idea is that you have to actually think about someone else. Not just grab a Dora for yourself and do something else as an afterthought."

"So if I gave this Dora away now, it wouldn't count?"

"Right," Emmy said.

"Thank God," Diana says. "I really like me some Dora." She looked at us defiantly.

"So what the hell, Chip?" Emmy said.

"It's just . . . I knew I could win that one. And it's like . . . it makes me feel good like nothing else does. I just get kind of lost, you know what I mean? I can forget myself for a while. It's the only thing that works."

"I hear you," Tracy said. "I get this buzz off of convincing people of stupid stuff that I am actually really craving ."

"Yeah," Diana said. "I used to cut myself for that feeling. But I know what you mean."

I didn't, though. Even among a bunch of really sick kids, I was the sickest. Because they had escape valves—weird, unhealthy, and potentially deadly escape valves, but things that made them feel better. I really didn't have anything like that. Which was part of the reason I took the Tylenol.

"But we were all gonna try to . . ."

"I did try, Emmy," Chip said, and it looked like his eyes were filling up. "That's the thing. I did try. But I mean, if it was as easy as wanting to, I wouldn't freaking be at Assland in the first place. I mean, are you gonna eat every meal like a normal human from now on?"

"Well—"

"I can answer that," Diana said. "She's been thinking about how to burn off those calories ever since that dog hit bottom. She'll probably try to get away with not eating anything for three days to make up for it."

"That's not . . . I haven't . . ."

"You really need to work on your lying skills," Tracy said. "Nobody believes you right now."

"Okay," Emmy said. "So it's hard. So it doesn't happen automatically just because you want it to. Does that mean you don't even try?"

Chip shrugged.

"Deep philosophical shit," Diana said. "And boring as hell. Can we go see Jenny's pigs now?"

"I just want you all to know this," Chip said as we all began ambling back toward the livestock barns, "I want to be gaming every single second I'm here. Every step I take away from those games is hard for me."

"I know," Emmy said. "I want to puke really bad right now. You have no idea."

"And I got my eye on a little farm-fresh cutie over there who would totally believe I'm a redshirt freshman basketball player," Tracy said.

"And I am a weepy little bitch," Diana said. "Oh no wait, that's all of you. Can we please get the pigshit over with now?"

Jenny smiled and patted Diana on the back and led us back to the pig barn.

"Walk around for five minutes and meet me back here," Jenny said. So we all split up and walked down the aisles of the barn, looking at the pigs. They smelled, but in one pen I saw two nuzzling each other, and that was kind of cute, and in another pen there were a bunch of piglets sucking on their mom, which was completely gross, but the piglets were completely adorable. But, I mean, after you've seen four or five pigs, it gets kind of boring, at least from my perspective. I had no idea what Jenny wanted us to get out of this.

We all met back at the front of the barn, and Jenny started talking.

"I'm not gonna say anything else all night because I've talked enough, and I hate it. I just want you to know this: Every pig you saw there tonight is going to be killed and will die screaming. And these pigs here, pigs like the one I raised, those are the lucky ones. The pigs you don't see are the ones crammed into pens where they don't even have room to turn around. They spend their lives in their own shit and vomit, they get gross patchy hair from the diseases they have, most of them have broken teeth from trying to bite through the metal bars that hold them in, and oh yeah, they're all so insane they make us look healthy."

"So what?" Diana barked. "So we're supposed to all stop eating meat? So we're supposed to burn down the slaughterhouses? Why the hell are you telling us this, anyway?"

Jenny, true to her promise, didn't say a word.

"Uh, buzzkill," Tracy said.

17.

EMMY

AFTER CHECKING OUT THE PIGS—NONE WERE GETTING MASSAGES, playing soccer, or jamming out to tunes like Jenny's *Pigs Rule* list suggested they might be—we hit the hot dog eating contest. Diana was busy drooling over Joey Chestnut, who was probably thirty years old and just about as attractive as you'd imagine a guy who gorges himself on wieners for a living to be, when I spotted this tiny Asian woman stuffing her face right along with him.

I couldn't take my eyes off of her, and just like that any fun I'd been having at the fair faded into a familiar black hole of anger and futility. The lady looked like she barely weighed a hundred pounds, but she was chowing down like a Biggest Loser contestant before going on the show.

I quickly ran some numbers in my head: One hot dog was

around one hundred and ten calories. The bun basically doubled that. And here was this woman who, according to the announcer, would quite possibly eat over forty of them in just ten minutes. That was nine thousand calories right there. At that rate, she'd gain nearly three pounds in less time than it took to watch an episode of *CSI*.

But the thing was, she was still thin enough not to set off my overly sensitive chub-o-meter. And she clearly entered contests like this all the time, because she was giving Joey Chestnut a run for his money up there, so it couldn't be that she restricted her eating anywhere near as much as I had to. Ditto for purging: No amount of puking in the world would eliminate all of the damage she did as a professional eater. *How does she do it?* I wondered again and again, and kept coming up with nada. Zippo. Zilch.

It was like, nothing made sense anymore. Nothing had turned out the way I'd planned it. None of this was what I'd wanted. Though I tried hard not to lose it, I started sobbing like a complete baby. Everyone—including Diana, who came here specifically to get off on Joey's eating abilities—was all over me in a matter of seconds asking what was wrong. Even Jenny hugged me.

"She . . . she's . . . still . . . skinny!" I finally managed to choke out.

"Remember how you said I had to be one hundred percent, totally honest here?" Tracy asked.

I nodded and swiped at my eyes.

"Well then, no offense, but no one knows what the fuck you're talking about."

I took a deep breath. "Look at her," I sputtered, pointing at the Asian lady, who apparently went by the name The Black Widow even though her real name was actually Sonya something-or-other. "She eats. A lot. And she's not fat. I don't eat anything and I'm not fat either. Get it?"

Everyone looked at me, completely clueless.

I tried again. "If I ate, not even like that but just like a normal person, I'd probably be Moby Dick in a matter of days," I said. "And she eats like a lunatic all the time and is still a friggin' toothpick. Right?"

More blank looks. It was like one big silent *And . . . ?*

"It's not fair, none of this is fair!" I was yelling now, and everyone was staring at me, and I didn't care. "I can't starve myself forever, because eventually I'll die! But the minute I start eating again? I'm gonna blow up like a balloon, I just know it! And what about that picture of my tits? It's going to be around cyberspace even after I'm dead. The guy I sent it to never came back to me, not even after I starved myself way worse than his stupid girlfriend. But I mean, what did I expect? If my real mom couldn't love me, why would I think some popular senior would? It's like a genetic law. Moms *have* to love their kids. But mine didn't. She left me on the street in a basket with a note pinned to my clothes, like some gross old couch with a *free* sign tacked to it that if no one took pity on would end up at the dump. Well, that's me. The unwanted garbage at the curb. At least I got the pity option and not the dump, I guess."

I couldn't believe how much it all hurt. It was true physical pain, despite being all in my head.

"For what it's worth, I think you're pretty lovable," Justin said, a little smile playing around his lips.

I spun around and glared at him. "I can't believe you're giving me shit again when I'm clearly not in the best place to handle it! I thought we were past all that. You suck!"

"I actually meant what I said this time," he told me, the smile gone. "Seriously. You should know that I only tease people I like. I'm like a second grader that way. Dumb but true. And you want to know something else that's true? Back there on the Ferris wheel, when you were taking care of me, I think it's safe to say I realized you are one cool girl. Lovable. Deserving of love. Whatever you want to call it."

I turned beet red and shrugged. Justin looked embarrassed but pleased with himself. "Well, thanks," I told him, sniffling. "That's sweet. Doesn't change anything, but it's sweet."

Diana decided she wanted a turn at comforting me, too. I braced myself for whatever tough love she was about to dole out. "For the record, I know you're broken up about your mom getting rid of you, but let me tell you something. Not all moms are sweetness and light. Mine for example? She's a total asshole, not to mention an alkie and a sex addict. I wouldn't be here if it wasn't for her, not to mention the scumbag drug dealer she dated who actually just wanted a piece of me."

I looked at our resident tough chick Diana, and realized she was just a heartbroken little girl on the inside. "What kind of mother lets her boyfriend do that to her daughter?" I whispered, completely horrified. I felt like such a baby, crying over my weight and being adopted when kids like Diana had a real, valid, awful reason to be pissed at the world.

Diana shrugged. "One who's passed out cold most of the time. And don't look at me like that. I don't need your sympathy, bitches. He's locked up, I'm fine."

I wasn't about to argue with her, even though I thought we were all at Assland specifically because we *weren't* fine.

"I'm never going to be a mom," Jenny piped up, despite the fact she promised not to talk again this whole trip. "I mean, my mom's not bad per se, but she totally loves my stepdad more than us kids. Takes his side every time, no matter what. Like with Wilbur. She promised me I could keep him as a pet after the contest, but when my stepdad saw how much money we were gonna make by selling him, he got mad and said no. She immediately backed down. So instead of bringing Wilbur home, we brought home the bacon. Pun intended."

A roar went up in the crowd. Diana's crush Joey Chestnut had killed the competition once again. That dude wasn't fat either. Argh, the world was mystifying.

A slide show came on the big screen onstage, flashing practically pornographic pictures of the first-, second-, and third-place contestants deep-throating eight zillion hot dogs. The Asian lady came in third.

"God, for all I know, she *is* my mom," I muttered.

Tracy cracked up. "Now who's being racist?"

I pointed to myself like, *Who me?*

"That chick's Korean, Holmes. You're Chinese, remember? You think all Asians look alike or something?"

I tried to laugh but it came out a single hollow *ha*! The truth was, anyone in the entire world could have been my mom and I'd never know. I was just going to have to accept that fact and move on if I ever wanted to be happy again.

Jenny uncharacteristically had still more to add to the conversation. "Want to know another reason why I'm never going to be a mom? Because I couldn't even protect a pig! How would I ever be able to take good care of my kids if I can't even keep a pet alive?"

"That's it! I've had it!" Diana yelled. "The guy who molested me? Said no one would believe me if I told, and no one else would want me anymore anyhow, not after what he did to me. Emmy's mom ditched her in the street and now she thinks she sucks. Everyone here let someone else make them believe they're a bad person or a worthless piece of shit or whatever. And you know what? Those assholes can suck it. We're a pretty cool bunch."

I started clapping, and soon everyone but Jenny had joined in.

"What, no kudos for the kid?" Diana asked her.

"I guess I figure we'll all learn to live with our problems eventually, whether we do it on our own or Assland forces us to," she said. "But those poor pigs? Are still screwed. It's like Wilbur all over again, and I still can't do a damn thing about it."

We all pondered that one for a few minutes, and then it was like a lightbulb clicked on over Diana's head. "I got it, Jenny," she said. "Tracy, you distract the lady running the show. Make up some of that awesome shit you're so good at—"

"But I thought I was supposed to tell the whole truth today—" he interrupted her.

"Temporary restraining order on that one. It's for a good cause," Diana interrupted right back. "Jenny, you get onstage as soon as Tracy starts working his magic and grab the microphone. Chip, you can hack anything, right? I want you to take over the computer they're using for the slideshow right now and find the most disgustingly graphic factory farm videos out there. Once Chip's got that going on screen, Jenny, you have to use your voice for once. Say whatever it is you have to say about Wilbur. That's the whole point. We can't just sit around being sad or scared or pissed anymore—we have to *do* something about it instead."

"What about us?" Justin asked, pointing at me and him.

"You guys?" Diana said. "Oh, you lovebirds are coming with me."

"Where?" I asked, not sure I actually wanted to know. Not that I had a choice or anything. Diana was already dragging me by the hand and shoving Justin ahead of her with her free arm.

"We're busting those poor pigs outta here before they end up like that," she said, pointing at a passing hot dog cart.

CHAPTER 18

JUSTIN

I WASN'T REALLY SURE WE WERE GOING TO BE ABLE TO PULL OFF any kind of porcine great escape.

I was also kind of worried. Had I just told my skeletal friend that I thought she was lovable? I mean, yeah, she kind of was, but still. Was it going to make things weird? Yes, of course it was. Did I mean I liked her as more than a friend? Maybe, not sure, possibly? I usually preferred my girls with some fat deposits on their chest that indicated they were actually female. I just . . . I guessed it had been a while since I felt any kind of connection to someone, and I just got carried away. And now that was probably going to break the connection.

Well, at least setting some pigs free was going to give me something to think about besides my feelings, which, honestly, I was kind of tired of analyzing all the time. "So," I said to Diana, who was still clutching the Dora under one arm, "what's the plan?"

"Plan?" she said. "I thought we'd just go through and open some gates. I mean, right?"

"And which parts of that plan stop the angry farm boys from beating me to a pulp?" I asked.

"We're just kids," she said. "It's a harmless prank!"

"No, Diana. You're just a kid. Emmy is female and would blow away in a strong wind, so she's exempt from the beatings. But I am a sixteen-year-old boy. I am prime beating material. Who do you think the angry 4-H boys are going to hunt down and beat if he sets their possibly prizewinning pig free on the state fairgrounds?"

"You're so sexist," Emmy said.

"Hmm," Diana said. "I hadn't given any thought to this."

"You mean you hadn't given any thought to anyone else," Emmy said.

"Well, yeah," Diana said. "I mean, you don't have to be a genius to connect the dots with me, right? When the people who are supposed to take care of you don't take care of you, you kind of figure you have to take care of yourself and the hell with everybody else, right?"

"I . . . I have no idea," Emmy said. I didn't say anything. And a new wave of self-loathing washed over me. My parents never abused me. Why the hell was I such a mess?

"Ah, Christ, Justin's getting mopey again," Diana said. "Emmy, why don't you go blow him behind the fried dough stand or something—oh right, calories."

I was blushing, and Emmy actually punched Diana in the arm. "You know, I was almost feeling compassion toward you before you said that," Emmy said.

"I'd say you punch like a girl, but it's really more accurate to say you punch like an infant," Diana said. "And I don't want your pity or your compassion or any of that shit. I just want my Dora and to set some pigs free and for everybody to shut the fuck up. I'm obviously never gonna get the last part, but I've already got my Dora, and maybe we can take care of the pigs. I've got an idea."

Diana told us her plan. It made me kind of uncomfortable because it used people's compassion against them, but I guessed that probably worked for Diana. We reached the pig barn and Emmy went right and I went left while Diana waited outside.

I pretended to admire a really colossal hog for a minute. He looked up at me, and I tried to read his expression. It was really tempting to think he was saying he wanted help, or he was bored, or where does a hog go to get laid around here, or any of a number of things, but, I tried to remind myself, he was an animal. Still, it was tough to look into his eyes and not imagine a mind at work behind them.

My career as an aspiring pig psychic was cut short by a heartbreaking wail from the center of the barn. "Mommy?" Diana cried. "Mommy?" I looked over, and even though I knew what I was seeing was completely fake, it kind of tugged at my heartstrings. There was little Diana, who looked about ten, her face red and wet with tears, clutching her Dora and crying out for her mommy.

I wondered for a second if she was able to fake this so well because she had a lot of memories of calling out for a mommy who wasn't there, but I never wanted to think about that, so instead I just threw open the bolt on the pen I was standing next to.

"There you go, buddy," I said to the fat pig inside. "You're free. Live it up."

I walked quickly, but not too quickly, down the row of pens. Pretty much everybody was looking at Diana, so it wasn't hard to just flip the latches open as I walked by without attracting attention. There were hundreds of pens in here, and between Emmy and me we'd probably only be able to get twenty or so open, but it was something. That was at least twenty more pigs that would get freed.

I reached the center of the barn and met up with Emmy. We were ready to run out, but then I realized something: Our pigs hadn't moved. They could get out, but they didn't know it. Or they didn't care. Maybe they were stoked to be able to lie around all day and get fed and brushed and stuff, and there was really no way to tell them, "Hey, guys, this really isn't going to end well for you."

A woman with her long gray hair in a braid that went down

to her butt was leading Diana out of the barn saying soothing words. "It's gonna be okay, sweetie," she said. "We'll find your mommy."

This was my cue, so I started heading out the back of the barn. I was going to come around the outside screaming, "Lynnie! Lynnie!" and then Diana would break away from her rescuer and come running into a big hug with me (her idea, followed by "and if you try to cop a feel, I'll cut you open and slop the hogs with your guts") and I'd say how Mom had been worried sick, thank you kind stranger for finding my sister, blah blah blah.

Diana shot me a look under the gray-haired woman's arm. It wasn't hard to read. It said, "Why hasn't pig-related chaos erupted yet? What the hell is wrong with you idiots?"

I started heading toward the back of the barn to do my running thing when I suddenly heard Jenny's voice coming out of the speakers in the barn. "—what happened to me and my friend Wilbur. So enjoy your hot dogs. And maybe think about this: Hit it, Chip!"

I didn't know what happened, but apparently Chip had managed to pipe Jenny's voice through every speaker on the fairgrounds. The same ones that announced that the Flying Linguica Family would be performing death-defying feats of aerial artistry in ten minutes, or that the tractor pull was starting, or whatever. Only this time, it was the end of Jenny's Wilbur story. Followed by one of the worst things I'd ever heard.

"This is a slaughterhouse," some professional voiceover person said over whatever video Chip found. "And this is the sound of pigs about to die." The next sound was the sound of a hundred pigs screaming.

At the sound of screaming pigs, all the pigs in the barn went nuts. Happy as pigs in shit just seconds ago—they wanted out. *Now.* And some started throwing themselves against the doors of their pens. The doors that were unlocked.

Suddenly, pigs were screaming and running everywhere. And as the pigs went crazy, people started running everywhere, too. Including the kindly braided gray-haired woman who was going to take Diana to the lost and found. I no longer felt even a little bit guilty about taking advantage of her compassion for a lost kid, because she spun around from Diana and immediately went running toward a pigpen. Nice priorities, lady.

Without even thinking about it, I started throwing more bolts open on the gates of more pens. There was so much noise and screaming and running all around me that it took zero effort to be inconspicuous and walk down the rows, opening gates. And every time I did, another pig came slamming out, and there was more chaos. It was kind of fun. No, it was actually tons of fun. It was thrilling to just do something and get instant results. It wasn't some medication that was going to take a month to kick in, it wasn't a therapeutic process that might take years—you just threw the bolt and a pig came running out.

Slowly, calmly, I made my way through the zigzagging, running pigs back toward the center of the barn. Apparently Emmy had the same idea that I did because she was just getting back to Diana also.

Diana had a wild-eyed look and a gigantic smile, and she was raising her hands, one of which was still clutching a gigantic Dora, to the sky.

She looked at us, grinning, and said, "Now I am become death, the destroyer of worlds!"

Emmy and I looked at each other and back to Diana, each of us clearly wondering if Diana had had some kind of psychotic break.

"Jesus, you guys, it's what Oppenheimer said when they dropped the atomic bomb. I mean, I saw it on the Documentary Channel. Don't you guys know anything about history?"

"There's a Documentary Channel? Really?" I asked. Nobody paid any attention.

"Of course I know something about history. I took American History class. But we never got to the twentieth century. We spent an entire quarter on the Civil War. Do you want to know anything about Appomattox? The caning of Sumner on the floor of the Senate?" Emmy asked.

"Who the hell is Oppenheimer?" I asked.

"You guys are idiots," Diana said. "I was just exulting in the fact that we've unleashed terrible destructive power, but you clods totally wrecked the moment. Come on, let's get out of here."

We turned to go and got about three steps out of the Barn of Chaos when a squealing piglet came shooting out through Diana's legs. Without a second thought, she threw herself to the ground and grabbed the piglet, dropping her Dora in the dirt.

"Got an idea," she said. Piglet still squirming under her arm, she ran up behind some fat guy in tight jeans and a cowboy hat with a cell phone attached to his belt on one hip and a utility knife on the other.

She bumped into him, gave a loud apology, and came back to us. "Here," she said to me. "Hold my piglet for a second, will ya?"

She held the pig out, and I had no choice but to grab him in my arms. He was squealing and squirming and he was cute as hell. When Diana pulled out the tool she grabbed from the fat guy's belt, I got a little worried.

"Behold the power of the Leatherman!" she said, unfolding the knife blade from what looked like a big pair of needle-nose pliers.

"Jesus, Diana, what are you going to do? You can't slaughter a piglet right here! I won't let you! *We* won't let you!" Emmy shouted, putting her skinny body between Diana and the pig.

"Will you relax," Diana said. She grabbed Dora, laid her faceup on the ground, and, using the Leatherman, sliced Dora from forehead to crotch. "There. I think that's just about enough space for our chubby friend," she said, folding up the knife.

"Don't worry, Emmy, I'm talking about the pig. Give him to me, will you, Justin?"

I handed the pig back to Diana, and she swaddled him inside of Dora. "I mean, you might get stopped trying to walk out with a pig under your arm, but nobody's going to stop a precious little girl with a big stuffed Dora."

"Or even a red-eyed psychotic hell demon with a big stuffed Dora," Emmy said.

"Yeah, that either," Diana said, grinning. "Come on, kids, let's go home. It's past your bedtime."

Cradling the Dora-encased piglet, Diana started walking toward the parking lot, where we all agreed to meet up.

"Wait. Why are you stealing a pig?" I asked.

"To give it to Jenny. Duh!" Diana said, and Emmy started to laugh. "What the hell's so funny, fatty?"

"You did something for someone else," Emmy said. "You finally thought of someone else. You sliced up your precious Dora to do something nice for Jenny, and you didn't even think twice about it."

Diana looked momentarily puzzled, then gritted her teeth at Emmy. "I'd advise you not to tease me about it," she said. "I do have a knife now."

"And a pair of needle-nose pliers," I chimed in.

"That should scare you more than anything else, needle-dick," Diana said. And then a really weird thing happened. All three of us laughed together.

"Let's get the hell out of this shithole," Diana said, and we all headed toward the exit.

There were pigs running everywhere, and people chasing the pigs, and other people chasing the people, and it was awesome. Kids were screaming in delight, pigs were squealing because that's what they do, adults were yelling, cops were running around: Pretty much all hell was breaking loose.

We walked out into the parking lot and found Chip, Jenny, and Tracy. "You missed it guys," Tracy said. "Lots of puking. I mean, a *lot*. They're just gonna have to hose the whole place down."

We walked back to the Assland van. The doors were open, there was terrible hippie music playing, and Tina was on top of the van on a blanket. With a guy.

Diana started making porno music noises. "Bwaw-chicka-waww-waww," she sang, and Tina scrambled down off the top of the van, followed quickly by the guy, a skinny-jeans-wearing guy with long hair and a big scraggly beard that went down his neck.

"Uh, hey, you guys are early," Tina said. "Wasn't, um . . . thought you and our fearless driver wouldn't be back for another hour."

"Yeah, well, we're early. Only so much fried dough and pigshit you can stand in one night, you know? Who's the King of Leon?" Diana asked.

"Hey guys," the neck-bearded guy said. "I'm—"

"Leaving," Tina said. "I'll talk to you soon."

"Can I ask you something?" I said. "I mean, isn't the beard growing out of the neck kind of gross? I mean, how do guys like that get girls?"

"Not—um. Boundaries. Professionalism," Tina said.

Tracy grinned. "Those are nouns, Tina. We need a verb in there somewhere for it to be a complete sentence."

Tina sighed. "Okay. How about this. I'll call Jeff to drive us home, and let's just go back to school. You don't ask me anything else about what you saw and I will pretend I think the sound of approaching sirens has nothing to do with you. Deal?"

"Deal," we all said. We climbed into the van to wait for Jeff, or, as I still thought of him, Not Tiny, figuring it would probably be better to not be visible when the cops showed up, and Diana said, "Hey, Jenny, I got you a big Dora."

Jenny scowled at Diana, but then she saw the piglet nestled inside the big-headed cartoon star, and she grabbed it and pulled it close. She didn't say anything, but she started to cry.

I wanted to hear all about how Chip and Tracy and Jenny pulled their caper off, and I wanted to brag about all the chaos we unleashed at the pig barn, but that was all going to have to wait until we were away from prying ears.

Not Tiny showed up, looked at us with his usual surly suspicion, and started driving us back to Assland. I looked out the window and saw black nothingness. There were probably cornfields out there. I was totally wired from adrenaline, but I guess a lot of other people were pretty beat, because I could hear snoring within about ten minutes, and a few minutes after that, Emmy's head flopped against my shoulder. I didn't know if she was asleep or not, and I didn't care. I looked out at the darkness and smiled.

19.

EMMY

I WOKE UP WITH A START AND REALIZED I'D BEEN DROOLING ON Justin's shoulder for God knows how long.

"Sorry 'bout that," I mumbled, wiping my mouth with my sleeve. "I guess the Whopping Wiener also puts people into a whopping coma."

"No problem." He was still smiling, peering out the window somewhere into the blackness.

"Why Mr. Sunshine all of a sudden?" I asked. I was used to Justin being Mr. Heckle, Mr. Grumpy, Mr. Mopey, and Mr. Angry. But Mr. Content and Peaceful? It was certainly different.

"I was just thinking how fucking awesome that pig frenzy was. Like, we created some major mayhem and I don't even have to pretend to feel bad about it because we did it for a good reason, right?"

A little snort came from the seat behind us, so I turned around to see what was up. Diana and Jenny were vying for the attention of the little piglet that was resting on the seat between them inside the eviscerated doll. The cutest little snout I'd ever seen was poking out from around Dora's tool belt.

"Man, that was epic, wasn't it?" Diana said, followed by positively angelic-sounding giggles. It was like our caper had turned her back into a little kid, the one she might have been before all that bad crap happened to her.

"Shhhhhh!" I warned her.

The last thing we needed was to get busted now. We were lucky enough to have been able to dust that place before the cops came, asking any questions. It would be a total bummer to have to give up our little prize and get thrown into demerit hell now, when we were so close to getting away with it all.

"Don't worry," Justin told us. "Not Tiny is behind his plastic divider again, and Tina fell asleep with her headphones on before you even started to drool. It's cool."

"Shut up!" I said, looking for any accidental spit stain on his shirt. There was none.

He looked a little sad.

"Don't worry, I only tease people I like," I said, nudging him in the ribs. "I'm very second grade like that."

And then he smiled at me like Mason used to. It was great and scary all rolled into one. I almost thought he might kiss me then, but Diana busted up the potentially magic moment.

"Me and Jenny, we have a plan," she whispered, even though Justin had just assured us Tina wouldn't hear a thing short of a nuclear explosion.

"Jenny doesn't seem like she's in a talking mood anymore," Justin said, and he was right. She'd been totally quiet since her big speech.

"Fine, if you want to get all technical—me and Jenny have an *understanding*," Diana retorted. "I laid this out to her, and she nodded, so that means she agrees. We are going to share custody of Little Willy here on a fifty-fifty basis. One night in my room, one night in hers. Since he's still a baby, I figure he'll spend lots of time sleeping. The only thing we still have to work out is how to get enough food to feed him."

I'd never had a pet pig before, so I had lots of questions. "What about exercise?"

Diana snorted loudly, which apparently Little Willy found hilarious, because he followed suit. "What, you want to put a leash on him and walk him around the cornfields at Assland?"

I shrugged, clueless. Maybe Little Willy *would* like a walk in the cornfields. How would I know? "I guess I'm just thinking he might get a little bored being cooped up in our room alone all day. And he'll have to poop once in awhile."

"Bored, schmored. Geez, look at his teeny head. He's no Einstein. You honestly think there's a big brain in there?" Diana asked, then barreled ahead without waiting for an answer. "And just look at his cute little butt. Small ass, small poops, right?"

I stared at Little Willy and decided he looked very smart for a pig. Maybe he was smart enough that if we made him a little litter box, he could deposit his little poops there?

I changed tactics. "What about the Staffies checking our rooms, then?" I asked, thinking for sure this would put a kibosh on the crazy plan.

"Once you get level two on Monday, they usually don't do that anymore," she said. "They have too many level one newbies to worry about. So you better get moved up, Skeletor, if you know what's good for you."

I was about to protest some more when Justin said, "Oh come on, Emmy. It's gonna be great! It'll be our little secret." I knew he meant the six of us, but it felt like just the two of us and it was nice, so I stopped resisting.

On Monday, I did end up getting level two, just by saying honestly in class how I felt about being adopted. It turned out to be a mouthful that went something like this:

"Listen, I've got a great, normal family. I love my sister like, well, a real biological sister and maybe more, and my parents are pretty cool. So that's good. But I've spent my entire life knowing everyone can see that I'm the different one—not only is it obvious, but people say stupid things about it all the time—and it makes me feel like a loser and an add-on even though my family doesn't treat me that way. And something else really stupid that I can't help feeling is that I'm mad at my real parents for abandoning me in the street even though I get it that they did it because of the one-child rule in China and they needed a boy to help support them when they're old. Unlike other adopted kids, I guess I'm lucky because I can pretty much know it wasn't personal. Happens to girls every day in China. But it still hurts like a bitch. And the dumbest thing about being mad about being adopted is that I don't even want to live in a misogynistic culture like that and I'm happy I grew up here instead, so what's my problem anyway?"

Everyone had clapped for me and it felt great and embarrassing and then when I went for my one-on-one with Brittany, she'd hugged me and told me I was moving up. And then she let me call home. I told my parents the good news and they were so proud you would have thought I'd gotten into Harvard or something, and then I was allowed to talk to Joss for half an hour. I was so happy, I practically glowed.

The whole experience made me want to keep moving up levels. It made me want to go home. Even Simon's Rock wasn't as appealing as before. Like, maybe college could wait until after my senior year of high school, the way normal kids did it. I'd started to think maybe I could actually *be* a normal kid again.

All of which made hiding the piggy an even bigger problem.

Especially since it turned out that little pigs did not make little poops—they made piles and piles of poop, which they also sometimes liked to roll around in and occasionally, eat, and then poop back out again. There was also the problem of getting that guy enough to eat. He could chow down more in a single sitting than I normally allowed myself in an entire day. And while I had no problem sharing three-quarters of my meals with him, I wasn't willing to stop eating entirely (maybe I was making progress? If only I could tell Brittany).

It was getting harder and harder to sneak the food out of the caf and into our rooms, and we'd already had to get really creative (cutting an entire block of pages out of Chip's trig textbook to create a nook to stash Little Willy's meals in) and sometimes, completely stupid (me, Diana, and Jenny staging a protest against BLTs in the caf, complete with hand-drawn signs, so the boys could shove as many sandwiches into their pockets as possible while the staff gave us a little talk about how they appreciated the sentiment but we'd have to stop pronto unless we wanted demerits and a level drop).

Next problem: The stench in our room was becoming rather noticeable, despite only having Mr. Piggy half time and cleaning up his messes as quickly as possible. I think even Jenny, who loved that pig an insane amount, was grossed out by it. Plus, my only perfume was getting dangerously depleted and I couldn't figure out what we'd use to cover the smell when it was gone.

Plus, Little Willy was growing exponentially by the day. He was still cute as hell, but you could totally see that sometime in the not-so-distant future he was going to outgrow his Dora nest and our dorm rooms in general. I had no idea what we were going to do then.

I decided to ask at lunch, when we were all working out a plan about who was willing to give up what food and how we were going to sneak it out of the caf and into our rooms. "You guys, you know we can't keep doing this much longer."

Jenny shook her head violently.

"Seriously, Jenny? Our room smells like a Porta-Potty after Lollapalooza and Little Willy has already eaten three pairs of my underwear. I'm gonna be permanently commando by the weekend at this rate."

"Boo-hoo about your panties, but there's no friggin' way are we giving up the pig," Diana said. "He's the best friend I ever had. Laughs at all my jokes, snuggles up tight at night—"

"You're sleeping with a pig?" Justin asked, his eyes enormous.

"Not like that, buddy," she said and kicked him under the table. "I would say 'men are such pigs,' but that's an insult to our pig friends everywhere."

"I'm just saying—" I started, but Diana was all over me before I could get any more practical words out.

"You're saying nothing, other than this: *Oh Miss Tina! I had a total epiphany at the awesome fair you took us to and I really want to get myself back to a normal body weight. My stomach is still too small to fit all the calories it would take to do that at breakfast, lunch, and dinner, though. Do you think I can also get two big snacks a day to bring to my room in between meals?"*

"Oh like she's totally gonna buy that one," I said.

"To be fair, Tina thinks we're making progress when we end a group by beating the shit out of each other," Justin said.

"Yeah, and she never catches on that my iPod activities are less than pure," Chip added.

"And don't forget, she picks up dudes with beards growing out of their neck," Tracy said.

A collective *ewwwwwww* went around the table.

"What does that have to do with anything?" I asked, but was drowned out by Diana yet again.

"The bottom line is you really have no excuse, Bones. You're the key to Little Willy's survival here at Assland."

Everyone else nodded. I knew I was defeated. "Fine." I sighed.

So after group that afternoon, I walked up to Tina and said, not so convincingly, exactly what Little Miss Bossypants told me to say. And instead of being all like, *I don't buy it for a second,* Tina actually got misty-eyed.

"Oh Emmy, I can't tell you how happy it makes me to hear that! You're making such progress. We'll start right away, at dinner tonight. I'll have them give you a snack to eat before lights-out."

"Ummm," I said, at a total loss for words. Could the key to getting out of Assland really be that easy? Like, just say what they wanted you to say—even if you didn't mean a word of it—and your wish was granted? I'd have to store that golden piece of information in my brain for later use. "Okay. Thanks, Tina."

"How did she react?" The gang wanted to know the second I joined them at the dinner table.

"Are you kidding me? She said *No way, Emmy. You're a lying piece of shit!*"

Jenny frowned and Diana gasped. "Nuh-uh!"

I laughed. "No, she actually almost cried she was so happy to give me extra food to fatten me up."

"Dude, you rule!" Diana yelled, giving me a high five.

I liked that everyone was looking at me like I was a superhero, but deep down, I kind of thought I was doing a crummy thing—not just to Tina by lying to her, but to Little Willy. Honestly, it wasn't like I *wanted* to get rid of him. I liked him more than most people I knew. But the thing was, he was also a ton of responsibility. All day long, every day we had custody of him—it was relentless. It made me appreciate all the real moms out there.

Especially my own.

I mean, maybe things hadn't turned out exactly the way my

parents had planned, but for my mom to have to take care of me *and* Joss, two little kids at once? It definitely had been a lot of effort. I should probably thank her for that when I saw her next. Which would be at the end of the term. Which was coming up quickly.

The whole thought of Family Weekend made me nervous. I wanted my parents to see how hard I was working, to think I was really making progress. I hoped they would, worried they wouldn't. I mean, I'd definitely figured some things out already. Others, I probably still needed to work on.

Which became completely apparent when I walked into Brittany's office for my regular appointment later that week and she had a scale waiting there for me.

"Hop on, sister. Tina told me about your epiphany, and I want to see what kind of progress you're making toward your goal of getting back to a normal BMI," she said, all smiles.

"Why don't we wait until I've eaten the extra snacks for at least a week? That way, I'll feel like I've really made a dent instead of just a tiny ding in my goal."

As usual, Brittany believed exactly none of my bullshit. "Every little bit counts and I want to celebrate along the way with you."

She motioned with her arm to the scale and I stepped on, my eyes firmly squeezed shut. I hoped I'd gained at least a few ounces—maybe from the Whopping Wiener?—but I knew it was a long shot. With me giving up most of my food to Little Willy these days, I'd be lucky to stay even with where I was a week ago.

"Want to explain how you can *lose* weight when you're consuming three thousand calories a day, Emmy?"

Brittany plopped down in her chair and looked at me expectantly as I slumped down into her couch. It was going to be a long session.

CHAPTER 20

JUSTIN

THERE WAS SOMETHING IN THE AIR AT ASSLAND. I MEAN BESIDES
the smell of pigshit, though that was definitely in the air, too. We
were not allowed anywhere near the girls' rooms, what with the
sexual reactivity and everything, but even still, I swear I could
sometimes catch a whiff coming from their wing of the building.

It was also the end of summer term. Real classes started next
week. Precalculus. English. Chemistry. And US History. Maybe
I'd figure out what the hell Diana was talking about in the pig
barn.

And my friends were moving up levels. Kids weren't supposed
to announce they were running for level six to the rest of us—it
was supposed to be this great surprise when they got to leave—
but I suspected balance and wholeness were within reach for a lot

of them. Tracy was going by his real name, Diana hadn't jumped anybody in a while, Jenny was talking, Emmy appeared to be eating, and Chip wasn't gaming. Of course, we were all harboring a four-legged fugitive, which would probably take us all down a level or six if it were discovered, but, otherwise, everybody seemed like they were doing better.

Even me. Maybe. Max and I had been "doing work" on figuring out my core issue. Though of course I had to take issue with that. Ha.

"My core issue is that my brain is screwed," I'd told him last time. "I don't make enough seratonin. End of story."

"That's not the story that you're telling yourself," Max had said. "You've got a story you tell yourself that affects how you see everything. What do you think it is?"

"*Goodnight Moon*? This explains everything. I like red balloons a lot. This feels like a real breakthrough," I said.

Max rolled his eyes. "Hiding behind a joke, Justin."

"It's cozy back here."

"But it's not helping you get better."

"Nope."

That was as far as we'd gotten.

But maybe there would be a big breakthrough in time for the upcoming Family Weekend. We were allowed to go off-site with our parents, and there was a minor Midwestern city about an hour's drive from here, so a lot of people were getting pretty excited about non-Assland food. Not Emmy, of course, and who the hell knew if Jenny would be able to find anything vegetarian to eat, here in the land of grass-fed beef and corn-fed humans, but everybody else was pretty stoked.

And terrified. Assland's idea of a Family Weekend was something that started on a Thursday and didn't end until Sunday and included at least two big-deal therapy sessions with the parents. I mean, even regular teens didn't want to spend that much time with their parents. And we were not regular teens.

So, yeah, I was kind of happy about seeing my mom and I guess kind of indifferent about seeing Patrick and really nervous about seeing Dad. Because when I saw him, I guessed I was gonna have to tell him about how angry and disappointed he made me feel all the time if I was gonna achieve balance and wholeness. And the man did not take criticism well.

Whatever progress I was making toward balance and wholeness was not being helped by the fact that I was completely starving all the time. Monday dinner was typical. I could barely sit down before Diana eyed the baked potato with sour cream on my plate and said, "Potato. For Little Willy. Now."

I sighed and handed the potato over to Diana, who stuffed it in a gym bag at her feet. "You know, Diana, I am a growing boy. I need my calories. I can't starve myself so your pig can eat."

"Can and will," Diana said, and as Emmy approached with a potato, Diana said, "Drop the spud, chubs."

Emmy actually smiled. "No dice. I just had a grueling one-on-one session where I had to swear for fifty minutes that I'm not purging all the snacks I've been getting. If I don't put on some kind of weight in the next week . . . well, I don't know, but I'm going to wind up getting treated for some kind of disorder I don't even have—"

"How different can the treatment really be?" Diana barked, but Emmy continued.

"And more importantly from your perspective, they're gonna cut me off from all the snacks. So Willy can have half of what he's getting now or he can have nothing."

"Well shit," Diana said. She folded her arms.

"And that's another problem," Emmy said. "It's getting out of control. I'll be surprised if the custodial staff doesn't start wondering why the Dumpster smells like livestock."

"It's actually your whole wing," I said. "When the wind is right you can smell Willy's crap all the way across the quad."

"Not all the way across," Tracy said as he sat down and handed his potato to Diana.

"So you just tell them you're not puking, but you're using lots of laxatives, and—" Diana began.

"I am *not* taking the blame for pigshit!" Emmy said just as Jenny and Chip reached the table.

"Shut the hell up, will you?" Jenny said.

"Hey," Diana said. "You guys seem to arrive together to a lot of meals these days. Are you like, *together*?"

"Well, we were together in the potato line," Chip said, smiling, but Jenny actually started blushing.

"Whoa, somebody's got a tell," Tracy said. "See, Jenny, my boy Chip here, I've trained him well. He can lie all casual now. Of course, he's an addict, so he's got practice. But still, the boy is good. See, let's try it." He went into a falsetto mom voice. "Chip? What are you doing on the computer, honey?"

"Just looking at porn, Mom," Chip said, and Tracy cracked up.

"See, that's excellent. Because if he says he's doing research for school, that's just an obvious lie. But why would you admit to porn? He'll at least be able to hide the World of Warcraft window before Mom gets to the room."

"Are you gonna game when you get out?" Emmy asked, all serious.

"Well," Chip said. "I honestly have no idea. One day at a time, you know? I'm not gonna game today. Tomorrow's gonna have to take care of itself."

Diana did a little robot dance in her seat. "I am a recovery-bot three thousand," she said. "One day at a time. Easy does it. I will now recite the Serenity Prayer. I owe you an amends. I have achieved balance and wholeness."

"Shut up, Diana," Jenny said. "You shouldn't make fun of stuff that's making people better."

"But then what will I make fun of? Oh yeah, just the fact that you guys are totally a couple."

Jenny blushed again and clenched her fist. "Bring it, Fern," Diana said.

I turned to Emmy. "Fern?"

"*Charlotte's Web*?" Emmy said to me. "Have you ever read a book in your life?"

"Now, ladies, let's not do anything that's gonna knock us back a level or two," Tracy said. "Jenny, let's work on your lying skills. Really, this is a crucial life skill, and I gotta say I'm a little worried about sending you all out into the world so unprepared. So Jenny, are you and Chip a couple?"

Jenny looked straight at Tracy. "We've made out a couple times. I mean, it's not like we have long meaningful talks or anything. Obviously."

"Ideal girlfriend!" I said, and went up for the high five from Tracy, who did not leave me hanging. We really were making progress around here!

Emmy punched me in the arm. "Pig. No, you know what, that's unfair to Willy. Now wait, I'm confused. So, was that the lie?"

This time it was Chip who was blushing.

"Just be careful, kids. Don't want to wind up in Sexual Reactivity group with Justin and the other pervs. Then you might not get to leave," Diana said.

"Why the hell is everybody talking about leaving?" I say. "I mean. You're not like, all on level six yet or anything. Are you?"

"Well, I'm not," Emmy said. "Level two."

And nobody else said anything.

"Wait. Really?"

"Well, I'm only on five," Jenny said. "But I'm going to have a big breakthrough in therapy this week. And then level six. And then once the 'rents get here, I'm out."

"Wait. So. Wait. So people are leaving on Family Weekend?"

"People leave after every Family Weekend," Tracy said. "It's like an audition or something. You jump through the hoops right when Mom and Dad are here, they let you leave with them. And if you don't, it's back to the dorms. We were all here before you and Emmy. Didn't it occur to you that we might leave before you, too?"

"I guess . . . um. Like Diana says, I'm stupid. But at least I don't smell like pigshit."

"He's not lying," Tracy said. "No offense, ladies, but I can definitely get a whiff of that porcine funk drifting off you."

"Great," Emmy said. "What the hell are we going to do about this pig?"

We debated the fate of Little Willy for a while. Emmy said that the pig was going to have to go, and Diana said Emmy just hated the pig because of her body image issues. Diana offered to take the pig full time until Family Weekend, Emmy said great, and Jenny said no way. And then Chip said this: "Um, Jenny, Diana. If you get to go home after Family Weekend, who's taking the pig?"

Nobody said anything for a full thirty seconds. "Well!" I finally said. "Guess it's not just Justin who's stupid! Guess there's plenty of stupid to go around!"

Everybody glared at me and left the table. Little Willy's fate was left unresolved.

But I wasn't really worried about the pig. Mostly because I didn't have to live with it. What I was worried about was me. I was only on level two. There was no way I was going to be able to go home after Family Weekend. I mean, the only things that had felt good and fun since I'd been here were the things I wasn't supposed to be doing. I didn't feel like anything was changed or resolved.

Except this: I'd made some friends. I didn't have to feel like the craziest one in the room all the time like I did at my old school, but more than that . . . I liked these people. I like actually looked forward to spending time with them. So who was the genius who'd made it so we'd have to separate so quickly?

I was feeling pretty good about stuff for a while, but as soon as I got back to my room after dinner, I started spiraling into the depths I knew too well. All of a sudden it just felt like I was never going to ever have any fun again. It pissed me off. I opened a book and tried to read for a minute (I did actually read, no matter what Emmy thought. Just because I didn't read a stupid book about a girl and her pet pig and a spider who died. Okay, I saw the movie.

I just forgot she was Fern), but I couldn't think of anything. I wanted to smash something. Or someone.

Which was when Tracy walked through the door.

"Whoa, J, where'd that black cloud come from?" he said. "The one that's on top of you, I mean."

"The only thing black and on top of me is your mom," I said, and Tracy laughed.

"Okay. Good. So you're not completely gone."

This did get a smile out of me. "Yeah, well, I may not be great at lying, but I can crack a joke that'll get my ass kicked."

We didn't have anything to say after that. I mean, I kind of wanted to say, yeah, I was really scared of you at first, and I hated you for a while, but now I don't want you to leave. But you didn't say that to another guy. It sounded weak—like you needed somebody else, and guys weren't supposed to be like that, or if we were, we were only supposed to show that side of us to girls, and then we could pretend we were just faking it so we could get in their pants.

"So," I said after a couple of minutes. "Level six. How's it feel?"

"I don't know. I mean. Good. But not, like, I'm totally fixed."

"You gonna . . . like go back to regular school and stuff?"

"Not the one where I conned everybody with my fake drug business. Not really welcome there. But yeah, I'll be headed back to school. Not to be a little bitch, but I'm a little scared of that."

"Why?"

"Because I'm gonna have to try not to lie my way through it. I haven't done that since . . . like, as long as I can remember."

"Well, I'm a scared little bitch, too. I can already feel myself slipping down, and there's a serious chance my dad might just blow off Family Weekend like he's blown off most important things in my life, which would probably send me slipping down even more, and it's like . . . I won't have anybody here anymore."

"Maybe you should take the pig. Then you'll have somebody."

"Maybe *you* should take the pig."

"I can't believe you told a kid named Mohammed to take a pig. That's haraam! Unclean, man."

"Yeah, but you're not Mohammed."

There was a pause while he considered this. "Yeah, I'm not. I'm still not taking that nasty pig, though."

But somebody was going to have to. When we arrived at breakfast a couple of days later, we found a haggard-looking Diana staring at a plate full of bacon.

"I gotta say, I'm a little surprised you're taking care of a pig and eating bacon," I said.

"That porky little shit kept me up all night," Diana said. "He was, like, rooting around and stuff, and when I got up, I saw that he ate freaking *everything*. I mean, stuff I didn't think mammals could eat. And then finally at, like, four in the morning he crawled into bed with me. And I thought he was going to cuddle or something, but instead he just took a big crap at my feet. So this is my revenge. I managed not to kill him with my bare hands, but I am gonna eat his cousins and enjoy it," she said, defiantly chomping a bacon strip.

"Well, it'll be fun to see how Jenny takes this," Tracy said, gesturing at the plate of bacon.

"That's what Chip said," I said, and Diana mustered the energy to high-five me.

Fortunately, when Jenny and Emmy arrived, they were too preoccupied to notice that Diana was eating the equivalent of an entire pork belly.

"Guys, we've been talking all night," Emmy said, and Tracy interrupted.

"Really?"

Emmy paused, looked at Jenny, and said, "Well, I did most of the talking."

Jenny put up the *blah blah blah* hand signal, and everybody laughed except Emmy. "Whatever," Emmy continued. "Anyway, we've made a decision. Little Willy really can't live here."

"Tell me about it," Diana said.

"So we've gotta get him to safety."

"Where's safety?" I asked.

"There's a farm refuge thirty miles from here. They take in farm animals and don't slaughter them or anything."

"Um, great. But how are we gonna get Willy somewhere thirty miles away? Might as well be a thousand."

"Still undetermined, we've gotta brainstorm that—" Emmy

started to say but Diana interrupted her before she could go any further.

"We're gonna break out!" she squealed.

We came up with a breakout plan involving laundry and food delivery trucks that sounded really cool when we brainstormed it around the table and incredibly stupid almost immediately afterward.

What the hell were we going to do about this pig? It was making me sad. Nobody wanted him. I mean, yeah, he was a big pain in the ass who ate everything and shit everywhere, but he was just being a pig. He was born that way. It wasn't his fault he didn't fit in. I wanted to help him, but I didn't know how.

I was still trying to think in my session with Max.

"You seem preoccupied," Max said. "What's going on?"

"I'm just trying to work out a problem," I said.

"What's that?" he said.

I really wanted to spill the beans because I wanted to talk this out, but one word out of me and Willy got the ax or whatever they use to kill pigs, and I became a social pariah. No thanks.

"I guess, I'm just . . . well, you know, I've made some friends here, and I was just thinking about how to help one of them."

Max tapped his iPad. One day I swore I was gonna catch him playing Angry Birds on the damn thing. "Well, that's nice,

Justin, but you know you can't fix anybody else. Everybody's on their own journey."

"Well. Yeah. Sure. I guess I just feel bad for him. He's a pain in the ass, and nobody wants him around. But he's just . . . he's got issues, you know?"

Max looked at me for a long time. "Yes, Justin," he finally said. "I think I do. But why do you think nobody wants him around?"

Oh crap. He thought I was talking about me. Well, better than him guessing I was thinking about a pig. I decided to go with it.

"Well, it's pretty obvious, isn't it? His dad ran eight hundred miles away from him. His mom got remarried and popped out a couple of replacement kids so she could have a family she wanted. And then there's me." I tried to make my voice crack a little bit on the last part, hoping if I faked a breakthrough I'd get to move up a level.

Max didn't say anything for a full minute. "So. I don't know about you, but I think you've just identified the kid's core issue. Nobody wants him. Am I right?"

"Yeah," I said. I had totally suckered this guy.

So why was I crying?

21.

EMMY

ONCE THE LAUNDRY TRUCK/FOOD DELIVERY PIGGY BREAKOUT plan got nixed, we spent most of our free time brainstorming other dumb ideas. Every one of them came up short. For instance, for all her quirkiness and semi-cluelessness/coolness, it just wasn't realistic to think Tina would drive us to the farm refuge herself if we confessed. In fact, she'd probably freak even more than the rest of the staff would because she was the one who took us to the fair and promised our parents we wouldn't do anything inappropriate while we were there in the first place. And, stealing the Assland short bus just didn't seem like a very bright idea. There was no way we could cover up the *Heartland Academy: A Caring Place* slogan painted on the side, so the cops would no doubt be chasing us before we even got on the highway. Besides, no matter how great any breakout plan we thought up sounded in the caf, it meant a greater than one hundred percent chance that whoever was ferrying Little Willy to safety would not be leaving Assland this weekend with their parents. And I knew for a fact Tracy, Chip, Jenny, and even Diana really wanted to go home (especially now that Diana's mom was supposedly working the steps in AA and SA, and they'd both be living with her nice grandma).

All this still left us with the stinking little piggy, and the question of what to do with him.

"Let's play a game here," I said at lunch as Diana was manhandling everyone's buttered rolls into a napkin and stuffing them in her gym bag. "Let's just say all of you get the go-ahead to leave, and me and Justin here are stuck with Mr. Smelly. What then?"

"Then you'll continue to take care of Willy until you can figure out a way to get him to the farm refuge," Jenny said.

I caught Chip patting her leg under the table, and I didn't even heckle them about it. It was like he just wanted to show her he was there supporting her, no need to freak out. It was so sweet it reminded me of . . . well absolutely nothing Mason had ever done for me. I wondered why I had ever liked him so much in the first place. Why I'd been willing to accept the crumbs of his affection when I could have held out for a relationship in which the guy would actually be seen with me. Actually be with me, talk to me, hang out with me, love me. It was exactly was what my next boyfriend would have to give me to earn the spot.

This place must have really gotten to me. Either that, or I was just so nervous about Family Weekend—which started tomorrow—that any stupid thing could make me go all sappy.

"Dude, get a grip. It's not gonna happen," I told her, my voice gentle but my words strong. "It's time for Plan B."

"Fine," Jenny said. "In that case, I'm sneaking out tonight after lights-out and hitching a ride there. Hopefully I'll be back by the time my parents get here. But if I get hacked to bits by some creeper before then, at least I know I tried my hardest to get Little Willy to safety—which is a lot more than I can say I did for Wilbur."

"But what about our plans—" Chip said.

Jenny shrugged miserably.

"Poor bastard really likes her," Tracy muttered under his breath. Justin nodded in agreement.

"You are not sneaking out," I told Jenny. "You'd be risking everything you've worked so hard for. I won't let you."

"You're giving me no choice," she said with a shrug. "Either you promise to somehow get him to that refuge after I leave, or I'm outta here tonight."

I let out a huge sigh. "Fine. You win. Again."

I barely got any sleep that night at all. Between all my tossing and turning and mentally picturing how the reunion with my family was going to go—and I couldn't imagine it would be anything other than humongously *awkward* for all of us—and Willy's snorting and rooting around and gassing up the place, I was lucky if I got ten minutes of sleep.

When I finally dragged myself out of bed just after the sun came up, it was like there was a weird current running through my body. Really, through the whole school in general. Jenny was already awake, sitting at her desk, looking green.

"You okay?" I asked her.

"I feel like I'm going to puke," she said.

"Welcome to my world," I said. She didn't even crack a smile.

"Seriously, what are you worried about? It's all going to be fine. You'll hang with your parents, they'll see how much better you are, and you head home with them. Easy peasy."

"What if I haven't changed?" she asked. "What if I just go right back to that bad place and stop talking again?"

I knelt down in front of her, put my hands on her knees, and looked her straight in the eyes. "You won't. But even if you do, you know you can stop yourself before any of it becomes a habit again. You've learned a lot here. You have a lot of tools you didn't have before."

She shook her head. "Well then, what if my *family* hasn't changed at all? What if my stepdad is as big of a controlling asshole as ever, and my mom still lets him walk all over her? And us kids? What then?"

I shrugged. "You know what they tell us around here . . .

you can't control anyone else's actions, only how you respond to them. You'll figure out how to stay out of their way. You've only got one more year until college, it's not that long. Listen, as much as I'm going to be lonely without you as my roommate here, I truly think you're ready."

The sick look finally drained from Jenny's face and she grinned at me. "Good thing you have Willy to keep you company then, right?"

I tried to smile back, but my anxiety about seeing my fam and the realization that I was going be stuck here all alone after Jenny was gone turned it into more of a grimace. By this time, though, Jenny was happily getting dressed and didn't seem to notice.

I witnessed about twelve sobby/huggy/apology-filled reunions on my way to Brittany's office, where I was supposed to meet up with my family, and it just amped my jitters to epic levels. By the time I actually got there, I was a complete wreck. Feeling like all the breakfasts, lunches, snacks, and dinners I'd been actually eating for the past week were about to come flying out my mouth.

"I don't think I can do it," I gasped to Brittany when I opened the door to her office.

"I *know* you can," Brittany said, and gestured for me to get on the scale. I knew I was expected to get on facing away from the display. That was part of the deal: Brittany didn't want me obsessing over the numbers, so I wasn't allowed to see them for now.

I stepped on and closed my eyes. I knew I'd gained weight this week. I hated the tightness of my waistband and the lack of control I'd felt eating semi-normally. My body, however, disagreed strongly. I hadn't had a headache all week, and I had more energy than since the end of me and Mason.

"Good, good," Brittany murmured.

I hopped off the scale and stood with my hands on my not-quite-as-bony-as-they-were-last-week hips. "How good?" I asked. It was like I wanted to torture myself or something.

"It's progress," Brittany said, and gave me a hug. "So here's the scoop. We find it's best for your first Family Weekend to have siblings spend a little time reconnecting before the whole family comes together. Kind of takes a little pressure off everyone to do these things gradually, you know? So your mom and dad are attending a parents' roundtable this morning. You and Joss will go to the gym for sibling game time until I'm ready for you all to come back here for family therapy after lunch."

I looked at my watch. That gave me and Joss about three or so hours to catch up and ignore the dodgeball game or whatever they expected us to play. And Brittany was right, it did take a lot of the pressure off. I was way less nervous and way more excited now that it would just be Joss and me for a while.

And then there she was in the doorway, all golden-haired and looking like Tyra should be begging her to audition for the next cycle of *America's Next Top Model*. I went leaping into her arms and she twirled me around. We were both laughing hysterically.

"I really missed you!" Joss yelled.

"Why don't you girls get on over to the gym," Brittany said with a smile, shooing us out her door. "I've got a Sexual Reactivity group to teach."

We walked in silence for a little while. I was feeling shy and weird about what to say, where to start my story of what had really been going down at Assland. Thankfully, Joss broke the ice.

"While we're on the subject of sex," Joss said. "I've got something here for you."

"I'm scared to even ask," I told her as she rummaged around in her bag.

"Here," she said, handlng me a big envelope. It was fat, like it had been stuffed with a senior thesis or something.

I opened the flap and pulled out the stack of papers inside. She'd printed out all my Facebook wall posts since I'd been gone, and they were nice as hell. One of my friends Lainey wrote a different thing she loved about me every day and had even gone so far as to start a *Bring Back Emmy Magnusson* group, which apparently had something like four hundred members in it.

"Hey, that was really nice of you," I said. "But I don't get what it has to do with sex."

"Did you read the bottom of page two?" she asked.

I flipped to it and sucked in my breath. It was from Mason. Saying how much he missed me.

"What!" I yelped.

"Right. They broke up again this week. Him and Lizbeth, I mean," Joss said. "I've been dying to tell you that."

Before I came to Assland, I probably would've hoped that meant we were going to get back together. Now, it just made me think he was a total ass.

"Now go to the top of page three," Joss said.

It was from none other than Danny Schwartz. *Sorry. I'm sure you are, too. I told the school no apologies necessary. Hope you come back to Stonebridge Country Day soon.* Lots of people had liked his comment.

"So, what do you think?" Joss asked with a huge smile.

"I think I want to talk about something else." It was just too embarrassing to admit how happy it all made me. "Tell me more about what's been going on at home."

She rummaged around in her bag some more and came up with car keys, jingling them just inches away from my face. "Got my permit yesterday. Mom and Dad even let me drive part of the way here. See? The car's right over there."

I noted where it was, then we headed to the gym doors. A ball immediately went whizzing by my face but I didn't even flinch— because I was having the best brainstorm ever.

"Joss, would you do something for me, even if I don't have time to fill you in on all the details right now?"

She looked skeptical. "I guess, as long as you promise me no one gets hurt—especially you."

"Promise," I said, grabbing her keys and her hand. "Come on, let's go. I'll explain on the way."

"Whaaaa?" she said.

I shook my head and put a finger to my lips. "We need to leave now if we want to get back in time for the stuff with Mom and Dad. My goal is to not get a level drop for what we're about to do."

We bumped into Justin right as we were heading out the door.

"I forgot what maniacs these dudes are," he said, gesturing to his twin brothers.

"I'm taking Little Willy to the refuge now," I whispered to him. "Cover for me and my sister, okay?"

"Wait," he said, grabbing my sleeve as I turned to go.

"What?"

"Let me help," he said. "I've been part of this since the beginning, and if you're going to put your ass on the line for Jenny, I should, too."

I shook my head. "We got this."

"I *want* to. Please," he said.

I looked at the twins. "What about them?"

Justin thought about that for a second. "Maybe your sister can stay here, babysit them and cover for us at the same time?"

"Sure," Joss said, and gathered the boys to her like she had a great secret. "Your brother and my sister have to go to a special class right now, so I'm gonna play with you all morning, okay?"

CHAPTER 22

JUSTIN

I GOT TO BE THE GETAWAY DRIVER. THIS WOULD HAVE BEEN COOL if I weren't behind the wheel of a freaking Honda Odyssey. It was pretty hard to feel like the main character in *Grand Theft Auto: Assland* when you were the wheelman for a rolling toaster.

I sat behind the wheel feeling like every window in Assland was hiding a person who was staring down at me. Finally I saw movement out of the corner of my eye—it was Emmy, small to begin with and now positively Smurf-like as she was all curled over and ducking behind cars.

She'd borrowed one of my jackets. Since it was big enough to fit a normal-sized person, it provided plenty of room for Emmy to tuck an increasingly large, bigger-than-a-stuffed-Dora pig underneath and hunch her way through the parking lot. I hit the button and the side door slid open—so maybe there were some advantages to using a minivan as a getaway car—and Emmy and Willy tumbled in. I hit the button again and gunned it out of the parking lot before Emmy could even sit up.

"Ah, Jesus, relax, will you? Nobody's following us! It's not like we just robbed a bank!"

"Don't wreck my Bonnie and Clyde buzz," I said as we turned from the gravel driveway out onto Rural Route 12. Emmy joined me in the front seat and started punching the Farm Asylum address into the GPS. "Hey," I said. "Won't they be able to track us with that?"

She gave me a quick, disgusted look. "Dude. We're only going thirty miles. Even on a road like this, that's still only going to be like an hour. They won't even know we're missing for another half an hour at least. It's not like we're going on some coast-to-coast crime spree."

"I knew that. I just . . . I wanted to be careful. I left a note on Mom's windshield just to throw them off the scent."

"Oh God. What did you say?"

What I'd actually written was *Hey, Mom & Patrick. Stole away with my new girlfriend. Needed some alone time. You know, hormones, sexual reactivity, all that. Sorry, but a kid's gotta obey his urges sometimes. Back for therapy and punishment tonight!*

But maybe Emmy didn't need to know all that. "Let's just say I won't be getting out of SR group anytime soon." Emmy yowled and punched my arm. "Hey! Not while I'm driving, okay?"

"Fine," she said. "Pull over so I can beat the crap out of you."

I didn't look over to see if she was serious. I just kept my eyes on the road and said, "Look. We have to keep Willy's existence secret. Right? I mean, if anybody finds out about him, they're gonna wonder exactly what he was doing at Assland. And that's gonna implicate at least Jenny, but possibly everybody else, too. And then everybody gets knocked back a level or three and nobody gets to go home. As much as I want them to stay, I don't feel like we can really do that to them."

Emmy didn't say anything for a minute, and then uttered a soft, "Dammit."

"What?"

"You're right. It's the most believable excuse. It's so believable that no matter what we said, people would assume we snuck off to have sex. Dammit."

"Well, you know, if you want to make it more credible, we could—"

"Yeah, with Willy and his funk in the backseat. That's hot."

"So it would be within the realm of possibility if Willy weren't in the backseat?"

She punched me again. "I don't give a shit if you're driving. And no. Not within the realm of possibility. You wish."

I stared at the road for a minute. "I mean," I said, "kind of, yeah. Not like . . . I mean, I just . . . like you. Like that. In the *I want to be your boyfriend* way."

Emmy didn't say anything, so I looked over at her. She had her eyes closed, and she was taking deep breaths. Only a few seconds went by, probably, but they went incredibly slowly. Finally she turned to me and sighed.

"Aw, crap," I said. "The like-you-as-a-friend speech. Ugh, I'm sorry, you don't have to say it. I'm familiar with it, and I'm sorry I brought it up and made the pig theft awkward and everything, and if it's not too awkward to still be friends, I actually do still want to be friends. Okay?"

"Not at all what I was going to say," Emmy said. "What I was *going* to say is that I think my mind and body are both still too messed up right now for me to really let anybody get close to either one. But, in the event that I start feeling normal enough for something like that, you'd be . . . I mean, you're like first on the list."

My face was on fire. I didn't know what to say. She'd just told me she couldn't be my girlfriend. So why did the air in this Honda Odyssey suddenly feel electric, and why did I want to kiss her?

I was so preoccupied I almost didn't see the Audi TT whiz past us at about twenty miles per hour over the speed limit. "Son of a bitch," I said.

"Nice," Emmy said. "You know, this is what I mean about not opening up to anyone right now, because I just put myself on the line and—"

"Oh my God, I'm sorry, I wasn't talking about what you said. That was incredibly sweet, and I totally get it. Well, I mean, I understand it. Sort of. But I was son-of-a-bitching about the fact that my dad just whizzed by in his midlife crisis car. I didn't think the old man was gonna make it."

"At the next intersection," the GPS commanded, "Turn right on Rural Route 25."

I did, and neither one of us talked for a while. For the first five minutes or so the silence felt nice, but then, after about twenty-five, it started to get awkward. I turned on the satellite radio.

"Oh God, my dad's classic rock," Emmy said, reaching for the dial.

"Hang on!" I said. "Look at the song!"

Thin Lizzy, the screen said. *Jailbreak.*

Emmy rolled her eyes.

"Come on! You gotta admit it's appropriate!"

"Fine. But after this is over, we're listening to something made in the last fifty years."

I drummed on the steering wheel as the song rocked on. I'd never heard it before, but it was pretty badass. And then I heard sirens.

"Oh shit," I said, checking the rearview mirror.

Emmy smiled. "Relax," she said. "It's in the song!" Sure enough, she turned the song down and the sirens went away. Almost.

"Ha, ha. Funny. Turn it off."

"I did!" she yelled. I looked over at her face. She looked serious. And yet I could still hear a siren.

"Think it's for us?" I said.

"Can't take the chance," she said. "Gun it. Hold on, Willy!"

I pushed the accelerator to the floor and watched as the speedometer crept up to seventy-five. This didn't feel incredibly safe, or, actually, safe at all, on a two-lane rural road. But we were still ten miles from the farm refuge.

I drove for five minutes, my foot heavy on the accelerator and sweat dripping down my face. I checked the rearview mirror obsessively and saw nothing. Until I did. Way back—probably at least a mile—I saw flashes of red and blue.

"Shit!" Emmy said. "They can't be after us. Can they?"

"Well, if I keep going this fast, they will be. We've gotta get off the road," I said, and Emmy punched the GPS screen frantically.

"Okay," she said. "The interstate is just a mile and a half away."

"I think that's a bad idea. Once we hit the interstate, the state police can come after us. They've probably all got our license number. Hey. Do you think they're tracking us with the GPS?"

Emmy thought for a second, then powered it off. "Probably not." She turned around in her seat. "Shit. They're closer. Lights and sirens."

I was going to go to jail. Grand theft auto, grand theft hog, grand theft anorexic chick. Ugh. Well, I guess better me than both of us. "Listen," I said. "I stole the pig. And when I saw you with keys, I made you drive me and the pig. I threatened you with bodily harm, and what with my manly physique, you were afraid I'd snap you in half, so you went along with it."

"Dude. What the hell are you talking about?"

"I'm talking about the story we tell the cops. No reason for us both to get locked up."

"Aw, Justin, are you trying to take the fall for me?"

"Well. Yeah."

"That's really sweet," she said, and then she started to laugh.

"Um. Are you laughing at the fast approach of the long arm of the law, or what?"

"No," she said. "I'm just laughing at my life. If you'd told me six months ago that I'd be touched because a guy offered to take the blame for the car and livestock I stole . . . well, let's just say I wouldn't have believed you." Before I could formulate an answer, Emmy screamed, "Truck stop!" and pointed ahead on the left right by the ramp to the interstate.

It had a full parking lot, and I could see at least three other minivans. "Okay. Here we go," I said and roared into the parking lot. I pulled in between two other minivans and killed the engine. "Now what?" I said.

"Now we take Willy and get the hell out of here."

"Shouldn't we, like, try to blend in or something?"

"Yeah, with a pig under our arm. We'll fit right in. And truck stops are the sketchiest places on the face of the earth. Some evil truck stop pimp would probably have us both turning tricks in the parking lot within about ten minutes."

"Evil truck stop pimp?"

"They exist. It's a thing. Now come on. That cop will be here in seconds. We've gotta find a place to hide."

I looked around the parking lot. I guessed we could break into another car, but then there was always the risk of the owners coming back. "There," I said, pointing.

"No," Emmy said.

"Come on. Let's ask Willy. You know he'd love it."

"God. I cannot believe the stuff I am doing for this pig. Let's do it," she said. She grabbed Willy, and we ran out of the door and across the parking lot and climbed into the Dumpster. It was exactly as nasty as I imagined a truck stop Dumpster might be. And Willy immediately started tearing through plastic bags and rooting around and eating whatever he could get his snout on.

"If I get through this without vomiting, it's gonna be some kind of miracle," Emmy said.

"So," I said. "Come here often?"

Emmy rolled her eyes. "Just keep quiet for a few minutes until the cops go away."

I pointed at Willy. "Tell *him*, will ya?"

"They'll think he's a rat."

We spent ten minutes sitting in the Dumpster. Willy was as happy as a pig in a Dumpster full of garbage, but I was kind of grossed out. Things were dripping on me, and it smelled like sour milk and piss in there.

"All right," I said. "I'd rather be locked up than stay in here for one more minute. Stay here and I'll check to see if it's all clear."

"The hell with that. I am going to projectile heave until I drop dead if I don't get out of here. Let's go. Come on, Willy."

Emmy grabbed Willy and we climbed out of the Dumpster. I didn't see any evidence of a police car. "Should we go back to the car?" I whispered.

"Too dangerous," she said, "they might be waiting for us on the road. We're gonna have to go cross-country. We're only a couple of miles away from the refuge. This way. I checked it all out on the GPS before I powered it down," she said and scampered into the tall grass beyond the edge of the parking lot.

And now I was the one snickering. "What is it?" Emmy asked.

"Pig on the lam!" I said.

Emmy rolled her eyes. "If you keep saying corny crap, this walk is going to be even longer," she said.

23.

EMMY

THE FARM ASYLUM—OR AT LEAST THE PLACE I ASSUMED WAS THE Farm Asylum based on what I'd seen earlier on the GPS—was a little speck at the end of the field.

"Let's make a run for it," Justin said. He was holding a grunting and squealing Little Willy under one arm and grabbing my hand and dragging me into the cornfield with the other.

"If Willy doesn't stop squealing, he'll lead the cops right to us no matter how fast we run." I kicked a stalk and then grabbed my shin. Those things were harder than they looked. "And getting hauled back to Assland by the po-po is not the way to get out of there anytime soon."

"Sometimes I wonder if I even want to get out anytime soon—" Justin began, but couldn't finish his thought because

Willy shrieked his little head off and wriggled out from under his arm. Willy fell with a plop to the ground and we both gasped.

But he wasn't hurt, and started snuffling around the dirt and plants. "Go on," I said.

"Maybe this sounds stupid," Justin said. "But I feel safe at Assland. And even semi-happy sometimes. The real world—my real world—isn't really like that."

I got what he was saying. But I also thought it was kind of a cop-out. We couldn't live in Assland forever. "No one's real world is like that. You know what I mean?"

He melted back into his usual gloom. "You mean you think it's better for me to feel crappy all the time?"

I shook my head. "Not at all. I just think maybe it's time you figured out why you're depressed at home but semi-happy in the loony bin."

We started walking toward the speck that I'd pegged as the Farm Asylum, following the rows of corn. The plants slapped Justin in the face every so often, and he swatted them away, all annoyed. I guessed being short wasn't always so bad, because I was below the face-swatting leaves and forged ahead untouched by maize.

The corn was planted in straight rows, which kept Willy in line. He walked happily behind us like a puppy. Justin took a deep breath, then slowly let it out. The effect was something along the lines of a leaky radiator.

"Easy, Emmy. I always know what to expect at Assland. Wake up, breakfast, school, lunch, groups, dinner, study hall, nightly reflection. At home, I never know what's coming next."

"Hate to be the one to point it out to you, but in life you never know what's coming next either. It's kind of what keeps it interesting."

It probably would have been easier *not* to tell Justin how I felt about this stuff. But that was what I had done with Mason—like, I never explained how much us being "secret lovers" bothered me—and look where it had gotten me. So I thought it might be good for Justin to hear what I had to say, and for me to say it.

But Justin scowled at me. "Since when are you such a philosopher? And since when do you think you're so healthy? You still weigh basically nothing, you still hate yourself and your life, so who are you to judge me?"

"Not judging. Just stating the facts," I told him, his words landing with a thud in my gut. I'd gone for honesty and it had been received like criticism. Not exactly the effect I'd intended.

"Fuck off," he said.

"Right back at ya," I said.

"Cops probably weren't even following us," Justin finally spit out after eons of silence. "If you hadn't gotten all paranoid, we'd have Willy safe and we'd be back at Assland by now."

"Right, I forgot. Your favorite place on earth," I said, kicking the ground. A puff of dust flew up in my face and sent me into a coughing fit.

"And I forgot how mature you are," Justin said, mimicking me by kicking at the dirt.

Unfortunately, he actually kicked a clod of dirt up, not just some dust. And the big dirt clod hit Little Willy on his little noggin. Willy looked pissed at being disrespected like that, squealed louder than ever, did a little piggy freak-out, and hauled ass away from us.

Justin looked at me, then took off. "Follow that pig!"

I ran like hell after both of them.

Pretty soon, we came to the end of the cornfield. But we still hadn't caught up with Willy. He was a freaking speed demon. The *Pigs Rule* fact Jenny had quoted—that our piggy friends could run up to eleven miles an hour—seemed like an understatement. Either that, or Willy was especially gifted in track and field and was going to qualify for the next porcine Olympics.

We kept Willy in our sights until he stopped following our row of corn and took a sharp left. Then he was gone like pure vapor.

I leaned over with my hands on my knees. "I haven't run that fast in . . . I guess ever," I gasped.

We'd been at a full-out sprint the whole time. Since I started restricting and purging, I'd become an expert at running slow and long but sprinting was next to impossible. So I guessed that was another good thing, along with fewer headaches and more energy, I could say about starting to eat again: I could run away from the cops and after pigs faster. Normally that wouldn't have seemed very useful, but like everything else at Assland, this situation wasn't normal.

"Me . . . either," Justin said, gulping for air before falling in a heap on the ground.

I plunked myself down next to him and stared up at the sky. "It kinda felt good though."

"Burning all those calories?" Justin guessed.

"Nahhh," I said. "Well, okay, yeah, that too. I . . . just . . . whatever." It was hard to explain, so I stopped trying for the moment.

Justin pointed up at the sky. "That cloud looks like the bearded guy Tina picked up at the fair, doesn't it?"

I spotted it and laughed. "It does, kind of."

Justin's hand found a way into mine and I didn't pull away. "I hate to admit it," he said. "But you're right."

"About burning calories and whatever?"

"I guess that, and also this: I really do need to get my shit together," he said with a little laugh. "What kind of a mess thinks being in a therapy school is better than actually living?"

"A really awesome mess," I told him, and I meant it. The truth was, I really did like Justin. Like that. Even though I swore after Mason I'd never like another guy again for a really long time.

"Sorry I said all that shit back there."

"No worries," was what I said. But what I was thinking was *What the hell.*

I rolled over so I was facing Justin and before I could chicken out, I kissed him. He looked shocked for a second but then started kissing me back. We both closed our eyes and just kept on going.

It felt nice. Right. Like we fit together, instead of me always trying to twist myself into someone Mason would want to admit was his girlfriend.

We still had a super-fast escapee pig to find—and then save— and needed to get back to school before we got in any deeper shit than we may have been in already.

But all that was just going to have to wait.

CHAPTER 24

JUSTIN

WHEN WE CAME UP FOR AIR, I LOOKED INTO EMMY'S EYES, AND I got it. I finally got what they were talking about in SR group. Like, when I was with Caitl-/Krist-in back at my dad's place in the summer, my body felt good, but the rest of me felt kind of numb.

That was not the way I felt now. It was safe to say there was not a single part of me that felt numb. Hungry was more like it. Ravenous, in fact. Like I liked Emmy so much I wanted to consume her. Maybe that was weird. Was that a thought that noncrazy people have?

"We should find Willy," Emmy said, and I started to laugh. "What? What's funny?" she said.

"Two things. One: Willy has definitely made an appearance"—

I pointed down at the tentpole in my crotch—"And two, I was just lying here wanting to talk about my feelings, and you're just ready to move on. It's like, I thought girls were supposed to want to talk about stuff and guys were supposed to be like, whatever."

"First of all, I'm not like, whatever," Emmy said. "I like you, you like me, we're ready to go on *Barney and Friends*. Second of all, this particular encounter is not going any further than this because I'm not ready for that—don't say anything, I know I said I wasn't ready for this much either, but I was wrong, but I'm not wrong about the rest of it. But also because even if I were ready for that, which I'm not and I'm not going to be today so don't ask, neither of us is exactly equipped for this to happen, and since I've been eating like a pig lately, I'm sure I'm going to start getting periods again soon, which means I'm not doing anything without at least two forms of protection on board. Got it?"

"If mentioning your cycle is supposed to kill my arousal, I can tell you it's not working."

"You are disgusting."

"But you like me anyway," I said, smiling.

"I do," she said. She gave me a quick kiss and hopped to her feet. "Now come on. Let's find that pig." She started walking away, and I got to my feet as quickly as I could, which was not very quickly because there wasn't a whole lot of freedom of motion in my pants right now.

"Um, can we take it slow for a minute?" I said as I tried out different limps in an attempt to find a comfortable way to walk.

Emmy looked back at me and laughed. "You know, if that's the 'poor me, I have a boner' trick, it's not working. It does look funny as hell, though. And also, don't complain about blue balls. Every girl knows that's not a real thing."

"Uh. Okay." It was a real thing. I knew this because I had a dull but persistent ache in my groin like you'd get in the aftermath of a particularly vicious shot to the nuts. Seriously. I thought I might puke.

But I sucked it up because we had to find this pig, or our whole breakout was going to be for nothing. Well, not for nothing. Because it had already gone way better than I had any right to hope it would. Actually it had gone better than most days I could remember.

Even with a terrible ache in my groin. "Will you hurry the hell up?" Emmy said. I did my best.

"How do we even know where we're going?" I asked.

"We'll just head for the farm asylum and hope for the best," Emmy said. "Maybe Willy has some kind of pig homing device."

"Maybe you're nuts."

"Remember how Jenny's *Pigs Rule* list said pigs have a great sense of direction?"

I smiled. "Right. So how far to the asylum? The one with the pigs, I mean, not the one where we live."

"I think it's a few minutes up this way," Emmy said as we

emerged onto a dirt road. She reached out and took my hand, and we walked down the road in silence. I didn't know why Emmy was being quiet, but I knew for my part it was because all I wanted to do was scream, "Jesus *Christ* my balls hurt!" But I wanted to be a man about the pain, and I also didn't want Emmy to think I was trying to manipulate her into more intimate activity. I was a horndog, but I did have my limits: I didn't want a girl to do stuff with me because she felt guilty. I'd rather have her do it because she couldn't resist my incredible hotness.

I snickered at the thought, and Emmy turned to me. "What's so funny?" she said.

"Long train of thought that's not really worth following," I said, and we walked for a few more minutes in silence.

"I just had another weird thought, though," I said.

"What's that?" she asked.

"Just now, walking here with you, I wasn't thinking anything bad or sad."

"Me neither."

"That never happens to me," I said.

"I'm sorry," Emmy said. "I—hey! Look!" We'd just turned a corner, and up ahead we saw a big wooden sign with the words *Farm Asylum* painted on it. "Nice! That's it! Let's see if they have Willy!"

She took off running, and I followed her. The sign sat at the end of another long dirt road. We could see a big red barn at the end of the driveway, but after a minute or two we got tired of running.

My excitement and contentment were wearing off, and now I was just getting tired and cranky. I smelled like garbage, my nuts hurt, my feet hurt, and we were probably gonna be in a shitload of trouble when we got back. And Willy might not even be here.

In front of the barn there was a big wooden fence, and there, behind the fence, cradling a piglet I really hoped was Willy, was the neck-bearded guy we found on the top of our van after the fair. He looked up at us. "You folks lose a pig?"

"Well, kind of," Emmy said. "More like he lost us. How do you think he found this place?"

The neck-bearded hippie smiled. "Pigs have an amazing sense of smell. Even more keen than dogs, actually. I was just feeding some of our pigs when your pal here came—hey. I know you!"

"Yeah," I said. "We met at the fair. You were—"

"Oh my God," the guy said. "That was you. The Heartland Academy kids. With the pigs. We had the state police here questioning the whole staff, you know. They thought we did it. And now you've brought this guy. Oh crap. He's from the fair, isn't he? You are totally going to implicate us. We can't have him here! What are we going to do?"

"You're gonna take care of him! You're gonna grant him asylum, like the sign says," I said. "We've busted our asses to get our little purloined porcine pal here. We can't take care of him, you can, and we're not letting him get made into bacon!"

Emmy looked at me. "Did you really say purloined porcine pal?"

"Awesome alliteration, dude," Neckbeard said.

"So, yeah. You gonna take Willy or not?"

A young woman came walking up. She had her brown hair under a purple bandanna, and her faded purple tank top revealed a robust growth of armpit hair. She put her arm around Neckbeard's waist.

"Of course we'll take him. That's what we're here for, right, honey?" she said to Neckbeard. She gave him a kiss on the cheek and walked away. He looked at the girl and back at us, and we could see the panic in his eyes.

"Yeah, we'll take him," Neckbeard said. Since he'd been holding Willy and stroking Willy's back through the whole conversation, I'd kind of figured he would.

"So, uh, listen, you know that truck stop by the interstate?" Emmy said.

"Yeah?"

"We just walked from there, and we're kind of beat, I've got a killer blister on my foot, and we would really love a ride back there."

"So you guys get me questioned by the cops, then make me take your stolen pig, and now I'm your taxi?"

"Well, you don't have to drive us. We can go ask your girlfriend there. And while we're at it, we can mention the circumstances when we first met you. I'll bet that would be an interesting conversation, don't you think?" Emmy whispered fiercely with a wicked gleam in her eyes.

"Lemme fire up the truck," Neckbeard said, looking nervously over his shoulder at the retreating figure of his hairy girlfriend. "You guys wanna say good-bye?" He held Willy out to us.

Emmy took Willy. "Bye, pal," she said. "Be good." She held him out to me.

"Um. Yeah. Well. See you. I mean, not really. But you know. Glad you're not gonna be bacon or anything."

Emmy yanked Willy back and set him on the ground. "You suck," she said to me.

Neckbeard came back with keys in his hand and climbed into the Farm Asylum pickup truck. "Come on," he said. "There's only two seats in the cab, so somebody's gonna have to—"

"I'll ride in back," I said.

"We'll both ride in back," Emmy said, climbing up into the bed. "No way was I riding alone with that dude," she said to me.

We both sat with our backs to the cab, and once again she reached out a hand. Our fingers interlaced, and we rode down very bumpy and dusty roads for about fifteen minutes, until we saw flashing blue lights in the distance.

Neckbeard pulled the truck over. "I am really not letting the law see me with you, you know?" he called back to us.

"It's cool," Emmy said. "Thanks for the ride."

We walked hand in hand toward the truck stop parking lot, where two state police cruisers were sitting with their lights flashing and our families—even Dad, who I frankly had not expected to see—milling around Emmy's family's van.

"We're in some shit now," I said.

"Yep," Emmy said. "But at least we're in it together."

25.

EMMY

"WELL, THIS COULDN'T GET MORE AWKWARD," I WHISPERED TO Justin as we walked toward our parents, therapists, and two cops. "Unless your boner was still making you limp, that is."

Everything about the situation was so absurd—how we broke out of Assland, stole my parents car, got chased by the police, did a 5K through a cornfield, and stopped to make out at the end, all to save a smelly little pig—that I started to giggle and couldn't stop. Justin joined in with a more manly laugh, and pretty soon we were practically rolling around on the ground in hysterics.

It was clear from my mom's glare and Joss's furrowed brow and Justin's dad's crossed-across-his-chest arms and everyone else's frowns that no one else found this quite as hilarious as we did.

"Time to pull it together," Justin whispered back. "Let me do the talking. I'll take responsibility for all of it."

I shook my head. There was no way I was blaming this on someone else. Especially a someone else I really, really liked.

Our families were in two separate little factions—Justin's to our right with an officer and mine in front of our car. Justin and I took a collective deep breath, dropped our hands from one another's, and split off to go face the music.

Brittany and my parents and Joss started in on me all at once.

"What in God's name did you think you were doing?" my mom practically screamed.

"Scaring us like that," my dad bellowed.

"After all the progress you've made, Emmy," Brittany said, giving me a disappointed gaze.

"I thought you said you were done with hooking up for, like, ever after everything that happened with Mason!" Joss piped in.

Everyone turned to stare at her.

"I mean, hi sis! So glad you're not hurt," she said, mouthing *I'm sorry* at me.

"Care to tell us what happened?" Brittany asked. Her voice was stern but her arms were open, like an invitation. I knew I could run into them and everything would feel like it was fine again, even if it was only for a few minutes.

But also I realized that was totally not what I should do. Not even what I wanted to do, really. Instead, I threw myself at my mom, wrapping my arms around her and hugging her tight. I breathed in her flowery-sugary scent, tucked my head into the little indentation between her chest and collarbone. I felt safe and warm and like I was a little kid again—back when I never worried whether my mommy loved me as much as Joss or not. Back when I knew for sure she did.

I held on as tight as I could, for as long as I could. And it must have been as big of a surprise to my mom—and to my dad—as it was to me. Soon, my father joined the hug. Joss squeezed her way in, too. We were the peanut butter and jelly to my parents' bread slices.

"My beautiful star," my mom murmured into my ear.

And for the first time in months, I didn't think *bullshit*.

"I really missed you guys," I said.

"We missed you, too," my dad and Joss said at the same time.

After a while, our sandwich kind of naturally fell apart, and I was left grinning at my family.

"You still have some explaining to do, Emmy," Brittany said, breaking the feel-good spell.

I glanced over at Justin for support. He winked at me, and I felt a hot flush creep up over my cheeks and a warmth envelope my gut. Liking someone was so great and so embarrassing all at once.

"Contrary to popular belief, I did not bust out of Assland to have sex," I began.

"It's called Heartland," my mom gently chided.

Joss just snorted and rolled her eyes. "Yeah, right."

"Seriously," I said, shaking my head and wishing I could explain but knowing that would ruin everything for Jenny and Chip and Diana and Tracy. I stopped and started a few times before I finally settled for simple but vague-as-hell. "I can't tell you exactly what we did today, other than it involves living things and doing my best to keep them living."

"Emmy, you are not responsible for anyone else's life but your own," Brittany said. "If Justin is having problems, that's for him to work out with his therapist."

I stole a peek at Justin and he totally broke out into a huge smile that everyone, even Brittany, noticed.

"And I know he looks happy now, but having sex with him won't get rid of his depression if that's what motivated you," Brittany told me.

"I did not have sex with him!" I said a little too loudly. Everyone was giving me those *yeah right* smirky smiles.

"I didn't!" I insisted.

"So maybe you can do a better job of explaining what you *were* doing, then," my dad said.

"All I can tell you is that I did something great today. Something I'm really proud of, and I'm willing to take whatever punishment you want to give me for it," I said, and then added, "and it wasn't sex."

Brittany didn't look like she was going to let me get away with such an evasive answer but surprisingly, my mom was kind of into it.

"I'm proud of you, Em," she said, putting an arm around my shoulders and pulling me close to her. "I don't know what you did, or that it even matters at this point. What I do know is that for the first time in a year, you're taking responsibility for your actions and not just blaming someone else for your troubles. And for the first time in a long time, you seem totally sincere."

This got even Brittany on board. "Sometimes you have to take a few steps back to take a giant leap forward," she told my parents. "And I do hope it was worth it. Because you are back on level one—"

This of course meant a Staffie would be following me around all day, even to the bathroom, until further notice.

"—and you and Justin are on communication block for the remainder of your time here at Heartland Academy."

The first part of the consequence I could deal with. The second? Was a killer. Because it meant not only did Justin and I not get to be a couple from here on out, we didn't get to speak or even be within twenty feet of each other.

But I also knew it was fair, because those were the rules, and we'd broken them. I'd just have to suck it up and deal. And maybe, just maybe, they'd take us off of comm block after we'd moved up a few levels. It would take time, but I kind of thought

Justin was worth waiting for. "Okay. I guess I deserve that."

One of the cops came over to where we were standing. "Are you pressing charges?" he asked. He had a ticket in hand, his pen poised above it. Today must have been the most exciting thing he'd ever dealt with in this back-ass town.

"No," my dad said, outstretching his hand for a shake. "Thank you very much for all your help, and we are sorry for all the trouble."

"Your daughter should be the one who is sorry," the cop said, staring at me, then Joss, then my parents, then back at me with a confused look in his eyes.

It had happened a million times before. Usually, it felt like someone stabbing me. This time, though, I responded a little differently.

"Families are based on love, not looks," I said to the cop, finally using my parents' advice after all these years. Joss high-fived me, my parents beamed, and I felt like a lot of what had been holding me down went flying off into the atmosphere like a let-go balloon.

CHAPTER 26

JUSTIN

I WATCHED ACROSS THE PARKING LOT AS EMMY HAD HER REUNION with her family. I thought I heard Max tell me I was forbidden from being within twenty feet of Emmy. Because keeping depressed people away from people they connect with was pretty therapeutic, I guess.

Mom hugged me, crying, then pulled away and gave me this fierce look. "We'll talk," she said.

Patrick put his arm around my shoulders and whispered in my ear. "You're in some shit, kid. I'm gonna try to talk her down, but just be prepared. It's gonna be ugly for a while."

I looked at him and smiled. Nice to know somebody was in my corner. I guessed my cover story of sneaking off to get some bought me some male allies.

Or maybe Patrick was just extra cool, because the other male in the picture did not seem to be my ally at the moment. "Get in the goddamn car," Dad said through clenched teeth.

"Can I drive?" I asked. I mean, I knew what the answer was gonna be, but how often was I gonna get an opportunity to get behind the wheel of an Audi TT? Dad's answer was a glare that actually scared the crap out of me, so I climbed in the passenger seat and shut up. I was glad it wasn't a very long ride back to Assland.

"What the hell are you doing?" Dad said as we roared out of the truck stop parking lot.

"I'm admiring the exhaust note of the TT. They had sound engineers work on—"

The glare cut me off again. "I drive ten hours out here into the middle of nowhere, and when I get here, you're not here. Are you just trying to humiliate me? I'm paying for this, you know. Is this your way of telling me—"

"Jesus, Dad, it's not about you!"

"Oh yeah, sure. That's why you just happen to choose the moment I arrive to—"

And something snapped, and, fear of the glare or not, I started yelling. "Why the hell would it be about you, Dad? Who the hell are you, anyway? Oh yeah! You're the guy who moved eight hundred miles away from me! You're the guy who disappears and pawns me off on every other relative when I come to visit! I don't even know you! You're not important enough to me to want to piss you off, okay? You're just some guy with a sweet car!"

I guess if he really wasn't important to me, I probably wouldn't have had tears streaming down my face, but whatever. We rode the rest of the way to Assland in silence.

We had another family reunion in the Assland parking lot. Dad and I both slammed our doors and climbed from the TT with what I suppose were scarily identical pissed-off looks on our faces. Mom and Patrick joined us and stared from one to the other for a minute. Mom looked like she was about to say something, but Patrick placed a hand on her arm, and we all just stood there silently until Max told us we should head over to his office for a family powwow.

Across the parking lot, I saw Emmy and her family headed off for a similar powwow. We locked eyes, and she smiled at me, and I had something nice to hold on to through the meeting. She gave me the heavy metal horns hand signal, only with her thumb sticking out, too. I was a little puzzled, but I did it back. "Rock on," I said under my breath.

Patrick whispered to me. "Wow. Already at the 'love-you' stage, huh?"

I looked at him. "What the hell are you talking about?"

He looked at me and started laughing. "You really don't know? She just flashed the sign for 'I Love You' at you, and you gave it right back."

"I thought it was a heavy metal thing."

Patrick patted me on the back. "Well," he said, still holding his laughter in, "if it wasn't serious before, it sure as hell is now." He caught a look from Mom and fell back into step with her, leaving me in my isolation.

Except I didn't feel alone. Not like I did before, anyway. I had a little warm feeling from seeing Emmy across the parking lot, and I put it down in my stomach where the pain and emptiness usually started, and I felt a little bit better.

Mom dropped the twins off in the classroom that was serving as a daycare center for the weekend, and as we did the walk of shame down the hallway toward Max's office, Diana suddenly appeared, coming out of the ladies' room. She shot me a questioning look, and I nodded my head yes. She smiled, gave me the thumbs-up, and disappeared.

And then we filed into Max's office. And I found myself in a dilemma. If I told the truth, it would probably show that I was making progress. I was actually proud of myself for the first time in, like, ever. I'd done a good thing, I'd helped Willy get a future, and I'd connected with somebody in a real way. Apparently I loved her. I tried that on for a little while. I mean, I hadn't known what I was doing when I flashed the sign, and if I had known and had time to think it over, I probably would have thought myself into knots about what it meant and blah blah blah. But I'd said it. Or signed it. Whatever. And I thought it was probably true. And that felt good.

So if I could tell everybody what really happened, that it wasn't about them, or even me, that it was about me getting my head out of my own ass for an afternoon and trying to do something good for somebody else, they might have gone easier on me. They might have even called that progress.

But there was no way to do that without revealing the whole sad story of Willy. And then everybody would get in trouble, nobody would get to go home, and the nice, if excessively hairy people at the Farm Asylum would probably go to jail. And all their animals would probably get killed and Willy would become bacon. I wasn't like the greatest person in the world, but I wasn't gonna have all that resting on my back. I could man up, lie and take my punishment, and be a hero, or I could weasel out of it by telling the truth and have just about everybody hate me and have the death of a bunch of animals on my conscience.

I was thinking about all this when Max said, "Why don't you tell us what happened, Justin. The truth. Remember, it's important to tell the truth."

Actually, it was important to do no such thing right now, but whatever. "I mean, what's to know? We snuck off, we made out for a while, we chickened out of having sex, we came back. I mean, do you want the play-by-play?"

Mom sobbed, and I felt bad.

"No, Justin. That's fine. Why'd you decide not to have sex?"

I mentally crossed my fingers, hoping this would at least get me out of additional SR sessions. "Well, I mean, it was like the first time we even kissed, you know, and it just seemed like maybe it was a little soon for a step like that. Also, I mean, a cornfield isn't the most romantic spot. There's a lot of dirt and bugs. It's kind of a buzzkill, actually."

Made that last part up, but whatever. Max smiled. "Well, in spite of everything else that's happened today, this, if it's true, at least shows you're making some progress. But make no mistake, today is a big step backward. And the first thing you need to do is to hear from everyone about how your behavior affected them today."

Mom said, "I'll go first," and her voice broke and tears ran down her face. "I was just so worried about you, Justin. I love—I love you so much. More than you can ever understand until you become a parent. And I was so—" She stopped to cry for a while, then continued. "So worried about you. I just want you to be happy and safe, and I ... I hate not having you at home, Justin. It kills me. I cry every single day. And I was so excited to get here, and then you're missing, and all I could think was that I lost my first little boy because I wanted to help him. I'm trying to do the best I can for you, and I can't lose you, Justin." And now she was sobbing.

And if I'd felt like a hero for saving Willy and keeping my big mouth shut about it, I now felt like the lowest, worst piece of crap in the world. I started crying. "I'm sorry, Mommy," I said, the little kid name for her out of my mouth before I could stop it. "I'm really sorry. I don't—I'm just sorry."

She hugged me, and we both cried for a while, and suddenly there were tissues and water bottles next to us.

Eventually I settled back into my seat, and it was Patrick's turn. He looked at me and looked at my mom and said, "You know what? I think I'm gonna pass."

I felt relieved. I looked over at him. I knew he was worried about me and stuff, and he was probably mad at me like everybody else, but he took the chance to spare me some more aggravation. Maybe it was just because I was all messed up from crying and from feeling guilty about being such a shit to everybody who cared about me, but I just felt so grateful that he wasn't gonna unload on me, too, that I flashed him the heavy metal "I Love You." I'd never said that to him before. I mean, I guessed I hadn't said it just now either. I'd signed it.

He smiled and flashed it back to me.

And then it was Dad's turn.

I found myself getting mad. The hell with this guy and his "Boo hoo I drove ten hours" crap.

And then Dad said, "I was really worried. I wouldn't have driven ten hours out here today if I didn't care. Of course I was worried. Of course I care."

He sounded defensive. I guessed it meant he cared enough

to defend himself against the charges I'd leveled against him before. Which I guess counted as a victory, but it felt kind of hollow. He wasn't crying, he wasn't explaining himself, and, even though there was this long, awkward silence where everybody stared at him, waiting for the rest, he wasn't saying anything else.

Max gave me this look that I interpreted as *Now do you get why I'm always trying to get you to talk about him?*

And then he said, "Justin, do you have anything to say?"

"Yeah. I do. I guess I just want to say I'm sorry for making everybody worry. This was actually less selfish than it looks, but I can't really explain that, so I'll just say I'm sorry. And I guess I want to tell you for when you're like, talking this over and saying how horrible I am and stuff, that this . . . little adventure is like the exact opposite of being depressed. I don't—when I'm really bad, I don't want to do anything. Going out, breaking the rules, kissing a girl, all this stuff I did today is like . . . I felt alive. You know?"

Nobody said anything. So maybe they didn't know.

I headed back to my room. Tracy wasn't there—I guessed he was off with his parents somewhere. So I sat on my bed, all alone. I felt pretty good about today. But then I started thinking about what would happen next. All my friends would leave, except for Emmy, who I wasn't allowed to see. I was proud of what we did, but I didn't think I realized what it was going to cost me. I guessed if I had to do it all again, I probably would, but it wasn't going to be easy.

I thought about the next several weeks. How was I going to get through it with nothing at all to look forward to?

For the next two days I had more group therapy stuff with the family. And then they'd leave, and everybody else would leave. Life seemed pretty bleak right now. And then there was a little knock on the door.

"Enter," I said, and Dad poked his head in.

"Hey," he said. "So I've gotta go. Big meeting tomorrow afternoon, and I just can't risk the traffic. So I'm gonna drive through the night. Probably shave an hour off the travel time."

He looked at me like I was actually supposed to give a shit about his travel time. I didn't say anything.

"I brought you this . . . a little container of Cincinnati's best." He had a Styrofoam cube in his hands. "It's probably against the rules for some reason, so you'll probably have to eat it quickly, but somehow I don't think you'll have a problem with that."

He set the cube on my bed, and, even though I was trying to keep a sullen face on to show him what an idiot he was, I couldn't resist peeking inside. I pulled the top off, and dry-ice fog came rolling out. I blew the fog away and saw four pints of Graeter's mocha chip ice cream . . . my favorite. Best ice cream in the world. Best thing about three weeks in Cincinnati in the summer. And yes, I was counting time with the old man.

"So listen," Dad said. "You do what they tell you, don't get in any more trouble, don't get anybody pregnant, stuff like that, you'll probably get to go home at the end of next term. Or maybe spring term. I talked to your mom, and she said it would be okay if I pick you up and we drive the TT back to Mom's place in Boston."

"When you say 'we,' does that mean I get some time behind the wheel?"

"As much as you can stand."

Oh, Dad. Trying to buy my love with material things. Didn't he get that I'd rather spend time with him than drive his hot-shit car? And then I realized that a road trip to Boston was going to involve at least twenty-four hours of driving in the TT, plus meals and stuff. Probably the most time I'd spent with the guy since he moved out.

"Sounds good, Dad."

He ruffled my hair like I was some little kid. "Alright, buddy. I'll see you, okay?"

"Okay," I said. I didn't ask him why he didn't stay, why he couldn't put me ahead of whatever stupid meeting he had and why he thought anybody cared about how long he drove. He turned and left. I looked at the ice cream and realized I didn't have a spoon. I wondered how the hell I was gonna steal one from the cafeteria.

A few minutes later, there was another knock at the door. "Yep!" I said. It was Mom.

"Hey Mom. I'm sorry."

"I know, sweetie. You don't have to keep saying it. I forgive you. You lost your off-campus privileges with your little stunt, but they let me bring in some sandwiches."

"Where's Patrick?"

"He's back at the hotel with the twins. I told them I wanted some time alone with you."

"Ah, Mom, does that mean we need to talk about our issues and shit?"

Mom laughed. "No, sweetie, it doesn't. We're gonna do that all day tomorrow. I just want to hang out with my boy for a while. Here." She handed me the bag of food, and I pulled out a sandwich and some fries.

We ate in silence, but it didn't really feel awkward. I just hadn't realized how hungry I was until I smelled french fries. Finally, I'd wolfed the whole thing down, and Mom was only about halfway through her sandwich, and she'd eaten like three french fries.

"You gonna eat those?" I asked. Mom laughed and dumped them onto my plate.

I vacuumed them up, and then I remembered we had ice cream. "Hey. Dad brought ice cream. But I don't have a spoon."

Mom dug into the takeout bag and pulled out a couple little

plastic bags with a napkin, a spoon, and fork, and little packets of salt and pepper inside.

"Why'd you get cutlery for sandwiches?" I asked.

"You never know," she said. I tried to dig into the ice cream with one of the plastic spoons, but the ice cream was rock-hard from being in a cooler with dry ice, so the spoon broke. "Let's wait for it to soften, shall we?" Mom said.

And then the silence got awkward as we stared at the ice cream together. "Mom," I said.

"Yeah, sweetie?"

"Dad's kind of a tool."

Mom sighed. "I know, honey. That's why I divorced him. He really does love you though, you know."

"I guess. He's just crappy at showing it."

"He does the best he can. It's just that his best isn't really very good."

I laughed. "You got *that* right."

Mom laughed. We killed a pint of mocha chip together, and then she gave me a hug and left. "See you at the epic therapy sesh tomorrow," she said.

"Can't wait," I said.

A few minutes later Tracy came in, patting his stomach. "Steak dinner! I got the itis in a major way! So. Did you get any?"

I smiled and didn't say anything.

"Okay," he said. "Keeping quiet. I see how it is. Looks like somebody's *in love!*"

I punched him, and he laughed. "You're just proving it now. Look, he's fighting for the reputation of his lady love."

I laughed and flopped back on my bed. "Dude, shut up, will you? Or are you just trying to make me happy that you're leaving?"

Tracy laughed and sat on his bed. "Fine, fine, loverboy. Just tell me about Willy's big escape. You can skip the sweaty parts."

I told him the story, and pretty soon after that, I fell asleep.

27.

EMMY

"MR. AND MRS. MAGNUSSON, EMMY AND I HAVE BEEN WORKING A lot on communication," Brittany told my parents when we got back to her office. It was kind of annoying to have her talking about me like I wasn't even in the room. I mean, she was my therapist—I'd prefer she stayed on my side. "Specifically on learning how to express difficult feelings rather than having them come out in other, unhealthy ways."

My mom and dad nodded at Brittany, but their eyes were fixed on me like I was some weird museum exhibit: *Sex Crazimus Facebook Murderius Maximus*. I wanted to assure them I was the same kid I'd always been, but I realized maybe that wasn't true. That maybe I hadn't been the same since Mason. Since anorexia. Since all that anger and depression had settled into my life and decided they liked it enough to try and make the move permanent.

"But I'd like to do something a little different today," Brittany continued. "Emmy, I'd like you to describe how you think your parents are feeling about you right now."

I opened and shut my mouth a few times. Everything that was racing around my brain was not at all what I wanted my parents to think about me. "I'm sure they feel disappointed," I finally said, and left it at that. It was pretty self-explanatory. I had been quite the disappointment lately.

My dad looked like he was about to say something but before he could, Brittany jumped right back in. "In what way, Emmy? Can you talk a little more about that?"

I figured I might as well get it all out on the table and finally put into words what I was worried they might have been thinking for the past sixteen years. "Disappointed that they still had to go and get me, even after they found out Joss was on the way. Disappointed that I'm so obviously not like them. And especially that I'm such an embarrassment and I ended up here." I was practically choking the last few words out.

I stared at my hands. The room had gone completely silent. My parents couldn't possibly want me back after all this.

When I finally got the guts to look up again, I noted with horror that my dad had tears streaming down his face. My mom, I could handle this from—she cried over tissue commercials. But my dad? I'd never seen him cry until now. And I was the one causing his pain, which made me feel like the lowest of all life-forms. I didn't deserve them, or their love.

"Mr. Magnusson, why don't you tell Emmy how you're really feeling?"

I curled up my toes in my sneakers and gripped on to the edge of my seat. I hoped these useless and desperate acts would somehow soften the blow of whatever my dad was going to say next.

"I . . . ," he started shakily. He took a deep breath and tried again. "I just want to tell you, Emmy, I've loved you from the second I laid eyes on the picture of you the adoption agency gave us, loved you even more the moment I first held you, and have loved you each and every day since. There are no strings attached to my love, and there's no way you can break our bond. No matter what you do, you'll always be my baby girl."

He stopped and stared into his hands. I let his words wash over me, but I couldn't quite get myself to believe them.

"Anything else you want to add?" Brittany asked.

He nodded. "It's really hurtful to know you don't believe we love you with everything we have, Emmy. We've never done anything to make you believe otherwise. We've always treated you and Joss the same."

"Because you *had* to!" I yelled, surprising even myself. "You *had* to treat me the same or else people would know you regretted getting me and it would've made you look bad!" Even as I said it,

I realized it sounded kind of lame.

"Em, I think even you know that's crazy talk," Joss, who had been totally silent up until now said, a wry little smile on her face.

I looked away, a flush creeping over my cheeks.

"Want to know a secret?" Joss went on without waiting for an answer. "I've been jealous of you, like, forever."

"Now who sounds crazy?" I yelped.

"Yup," she said with a shrug. "You're the beautiful star, the one Mom and Dad flew halfway around the world to get because she's so special. I'm just . . . whatever came out, you know? You were actually chosen."

"Now Joss," my mother said softly. "We would've flown around the world and picked you, too. We wanted both of you, and we'll always love both of you equally."

Brittany was grinning from ear to ear now. I could tell how much she liked her job on most days, but this must have felt like a banner moment to her because she was practically floating on air. "I want to point something out here, mostly to you girls," Brittany said. "But it's a lesson everyone can benefit from. When we don't directly ask for clarification, we tend to fill in the gaps with negative thoughts. These eventually become rooted in our minds as truths, and then everyone gets stuck in a cycle of misunderstanding and miscommunication."

"We love you, Emmy," my mom assured me. "We're a family. All four of us. It's not three against one. It never was."

"I love you guys, too," I whispered.

"From here on out," Brittany said. "Remember to check out anything you're unsure about with each other, rather than just filling in the blanks with negative assumptions that most likely are false. Okay?"

We all nodded, and the session was over.

My parents hugged me and told me they'd bring me dinner later. I was exhausted. I just wanted to lie down for a while. I needed time to process everything that had gone down today.

Except when I got to my room, Jenny's whole family was crammed in there, packing up her stuff. Jenny started jumping up and down when she saw me, then dragged me into the least-crowded corner. "So you guys really did it, huh?"

I nodded, and she scooped me into a bear hug. "How can I ever repay you?" she asked.

Ever since we'd left the truck stop parking lot, all I'd been thinking about was how much I wished I could talk to Justin. But that wasn't going to happen any time soon. Unless . . .

"Maybe you guys could figure out a way for Justin and me to communicate without the staff finding out?"

She gave me a huge smile and another hug. "Consider it done."

CHAPTER 28

JUSTIN

THE ALL-DAY THERAPY SESH WENT JUST ABOUT AS WELL AS I could have hoped. Mostly because it didn't take all day.

My psychopharmacologist was going to stop by to make sure my meds were doing what they were supposed to do. And I had to journal. I got irrationally annoyed by the use of that word as a verb, but oh well. And in light of what they actually believed was responsible decision-making around my sexual activities, I didn't have to do the SR group anymore.

I was stoked to not have to hear about all the SR guys' emissions anymore, but otherwise, the whole thing was kind of a bust as far as I was concerned. There was no breakthrough or anything. I knew Mom and Patrick loved me. I knew Dad was a tool, and I guess I sort of knew that him being a tool wasn't because he was so disappointed at having me for a son. Not a hundred percent sure about that one, actually, but Mom assured me that he was a tool before I was born.

"So why'd you marry him, Mom? I mean, I'm glad you did and everything, because of the whole me existing part, but still."

Mom smiled. "Yeah, well, that's something I get to work out with my own therapist, kiddo."

And then it pretty much wrapped up, just a couple of hours in. Max said, "Well, I think it's clear that Justin and his dad have some things they need to work on together, and with him not here, we've probably gotten about as far as we can today."

That was true, of course, though I kind of doubted Dad and I were ever going to work on our things together. I suspected we'd just spend the rest of our lives trying and failing to pretend like we didn't have things to work on. Awesome!

It didn't really matter anyway. Having some big conversation with Dad wasn't going to make me better. This was the part that made me sad. I was just defective, and I didn't know if I could ever be fixed. Though Max assured me that we could get that little voice to stop whispering "nobody wants you" in my ear all the time. It hadn't happened yet, but that would actually be a pretty big improvement.

The next day after breakfast, Mom and Patrick and the twins said their tearful good-byes—well, it was actually only tearful for Mom. Okay, and me, too. I sat down to journal. I had to show Max that I'd been doing it, but I didn't have to share anything with him unless I wanted to, so I felt like I could write about what had actually happened over the last few days.

PROS

Freed Willy. Most, and possibly only worthwhile thing I've ever done. Felt good.

Made friends.

Emmy.

Realized I think nobody wants me.

CONS

Friends leaving.

Dad's a tool.

Emmy is off-limits.

Realizing my "core issue" didn't actually make it go away.

Ugh. Writing it down made it hurt worse. Awesome idea, genius therapist. And then it was time to say good-bye to all my friends.

The girls were allowed to come into the lobby of our wing since it was such a special occasion. So Jenny came in and gave me a big hug. "Thank you," she said. "Thank you for saving him. That was a great thing you did." I pulled away and saw that she was crying. Without even thinking about it, I reached out and wiped a tear away with my thumb.

"You're a nice guy," Jenny said. "I get why she likes you. Oh crap. I almost forgot. One last handshake."

I looked at her for a second. "One last handshake? Are you serious? I mean, who the hell does that? We've already hugged, but we should shake hands—"

She gritted her teeth and whispered, "Just shake my damn hand, okay?"

I reached my hand out, and Jenny grasped it with her right hand and then grabbed the other side of my hand with her left hand. And pressed a folded-up piece of paper into it. Idiot. It was a note from Emmy. And I was too stupid to write anything to give to Tracy or Chip to give to her. Oh well.

And then it was Diana's turn, and she came up and threw her arms around me and whispered fiercely in my ear. "You know what my favorite Harry Potter book is?"

"Um. No."

"*Goblet of Fire*. Got it? *Goblet of Fire*. It's the fourth one."

"Yyyeah. Okay."

"Say it back to me."

"*Goblet of Fire*."

She released me and ran out the door, tossing a hurried "see ya!" over her shoulder as she went. Weird.

And then Chip came over. It was always awkward with a guy—were we gonna shake hands or hug? He held his hand up to clasp mine, and when I hit him with the high five, he pulled me in for a manly, shoulder-to-shoulder hug, accompanied by a couple of slaps on the back. He also pressed something into my hand. It was a small piece of hard plastic.

"Left my netbook with the powers that be so you can use it when you get to level three," he said out loud, and then whispered, "That's a flash drive full of porn. Don't do anything I wouldn't do. And don't ask where I hid it when I got here."

Well, that was a touching, if kind of weird and gross gesture. A couple of gigs of porn from Chip was like a diamond from anybody else in how precious it was to the giver, so I tried to take it in that spirit. And let's be honest—it was gonna get some use no matter how much it skeeved me out.

Tracy came over and gave me a real hug. "Alright, man. We'll talk when you get out. If not sooner."

"You gonna write me? I don't see you as much of a letter writer."

"Nah, I just . . . you just never know what's gonna happen, you know?"

"I guess," I said, but I had no idea what the hell he was talking about.

"Take care," Tracy said. "And thanks for . . . you know."

"No problem," I said. He was thanking me for taking the fall for everybody else. I felt like I was in a gangster movie or something. It was actually pretty awesome. "Trace," I said as he started to walk away.

"Yeah?" he said.

"I just—you're a really cool guy. Probably the coolest guy

I've ever met. So maybe you don't have to be anybody else?" As soon as it was out of my mouth, I felt stupid. This was not the kind of thing guys said to each other.

But he took it well. He broke into a big grin and said, "Thanks, man. But you know, old habits die hard. Stay the hell away from the medicine cabinet, will you?"

"Yeah," I said. I watched him walk through the glass door and across the lawn to join his parents. They all climbed into an SUV and drove out of the parking lot. I watched until I couldn't see any of the dust they kicked up floating in the air anymore. And then I went up to my room to cry.

It was just about dinnertime, but I didn't feel like eating. I'd have to go eventually because skipping meals was not allowed, but I was gonna take a minute to try to pull myself together and make myself go. It wasn't like the Assland food was so awesome to begin with, but with everybody gone except Emmy, who might as well have been gone for all I was going to get to see her, it was going to be intolerable.

Thinking of Emmy reminded me that I had a note from her in my pocket. I quickly unfolded it, expecting to find it packed with words. But all it said was this:

I'm sad
And I miss everybody
But you most of all
And I'm proud of you

And I'm proud of myself
And I think about you
And that makes me happy

I really wanted to kiss this girl. Right now. But with all our trustworthy intermediaries gone, I didn't even know how to get a message to her. I read the poem again. And again. And I was still sad, but this made me happier.

A girl. Wrote me. A poem. A *poem*! Ha! I may have been defective and screwed up, and maybe it took a girl who was just as crazy as me to actually like me, but I didn't care. I thought about her. And that made me happy.

Of course, I did end up going down to the cafeteria before somebody came up to make me go, and then I'd have to have an emergency session to explain my self-destructive behavior. The hell with that. It was much easier to choke down some food. The buzz I got from the poem didn't last too long. The staff filled the transition day—the day after everybody leaves but before everybody else arrives—with a field trip for a supposedly fun activity that actually sucked: The nauseating, nut-busting horror of the high ropes course, which was not a metaphor for anything and which did not inspire me to want to do anything except puke and maybe soak my harness-cramped nuts in ice water for a couple of hours.

Who thought of this crap?

The only bright spot happened when I was standing up on the top of a telephone pole, and I was in the nut-buster harness, and I was supposed to jump off and trust the yutzes on the ground to pull the rope attached to the harness hard enough that I only got a hard shot to the family jewels instead of splatting on the ground. I looked across the course, and there, inching her way across two ropes that hung between towers, was Emmy. She looked up at me, and I threw up the heavy metal "I Love You." She threw it right back, then quickly grabbed the rope before she toppled off it. I jumped off the pole and was rewarded by testicular pain and forty minutes of processing the experience and what it meant in terms of my life. I told them it meant that I was willing to take risks and trust people because that was what they wanted to hear, but all I could think was, "This was the dumbest thing I've ever heard of, and you should have told me to wear a cup."

The new roommate arrived the next day, and I got to be the sullen kid sulking on his bed when the new kid arrived.

His name was Josh, and he was on the smallish side, with curly brown hair and freckles. "What you in for?" I said.

"Suicidal ideation," he said.

"Make an attempt?" I asked.

"Nah. I just wrote a novel in the form of a series of inter-connected short stories in which teenagers commit suicide. Therapist told my mom he thought I might try it. I wouldn't, but it got me out of the hellhole where I went to school and away from my stepdad."

"Well. Welcome," I said. And that was pretty much it for a while. I sat with the kid at meals, but it was hard to feel like I was connected with him, when all I could think is how he wasn't like Tracy or even Chip.

I'd started to get sad again. The note was now five days old. The heavy metal sign atop the horrible ropes course was four days old. And I had nothing to look forward to until the end of the semester.

Food didn't taste like anything, and every morning it got harder to get out of bed. What the hell was the point, anyway?

Max told me I could expect a difficult few weeks while they adjusted my meds but to just remember how far I'd come and all the good times I'd had since I'd gotten here, and that if I had fun once it means I could have fun again.

Maybe.

I mean, I knew he was right. But I was scared. I could feel myself at the top of the slide again, and I knew I'd gotten off the chute and found a ladder last time, but I wasn't sure I was gonna be able to do it again. What if I started going down and I never found my way up again?

Max said those thoughts were always going to be with me, that I was going to have ups and downs in my life like anybody else, and to remember the ups. There would always be more ups.

I didn't see any in the near future, though.

But then there was a knock at my door. "Um. Yeah?"

"There's a package for you," a voice said, and I recognized it as the voice of Tiny, the colossal guy they always brought in to tackle people.

"Tiny, are you here to restrain me? Is this some kind of gag you use to get into kids' rooms when you have to haul them away?"

"These doors don't lock, genius. Now hurry up. This thing is freakin' heavy."

I opened the door, and, sure enough, there was Tiny holding a huge cardboard box. "We had to open it. Standard procedure."

"I figured," I said. "Um. Can you just set it on the floor?"

"You got it," he said, and placed the box on the floor.

"Sorry I can't tip you, but, you know, they don't let me have money," I said, smiling.

Tiny glared at me and said, deadpan, "The knowledge that I brought a little joy to your day is all the tip I need."

And with that, Tiny was gone, and I was alone with the package. The return address said *Diana, etc. but mostly Diana.*

I opened it up, and inside I saw seven hardcover books. The complete Harry Potter series. I pulled one out. *Harry Potter and the Sorcerer's Ass*, the carefully altered cover said. And then I realized they'd all been tampered with. *Harry Potter and the*

Chamber of Ass. Harry Potter and the Prisoner of Asskaban. Harry Potter and the Ass of Fire. Harry Potter and the Ass of the Phoenix. Harry Potter and the Half-Assed Prince. Harry Potter and the Deathly Ass.

I wasn't that interested in reading the adventures of a boy wizard, but it was really nice that they'd spent so much cash to bring me something nice and took the time to alter every cover to fit in the ass joke.

I pulled them out and lined them up on my desk. And I actually found myself smiling.

The next day Josh said, "So is this cardboard box a permanent feature of the room now, or what?"

"Right. Sorry. I got it," I said. Of course we weren't allowed to have anything that might be sharp enough to cut through packing tape, so it took me quite a while to break the box down. When I finally got the bottom apart, a piece of paper fluttered to the floor.

I hope these will make the rest of your time more bearable. Remember my favorite? I think it'll really speak to you.

—Diana

I put the broken-down box behind the wastepaper basket and went to lie on my bed. I wondered why she thought the fourth book in particular would speak to me. I decided to take a look, though obviously I wasn't gonna start with book four.

I pulled it off the desk and read the flap. Something about a contest—not sure how that was supposed to relate. I flipped through the pages, and then I realized there was something wrong. Some of the pages wouldn't flip. I could flip through fine for a couple of hundred pages, and then it was like the rest of the pages in this huge book were all glued together or something.

I opened it to the glued section and smiled. It was all I could do not to smack my forehead. I was such a freakin' idiot. This was why she thought book four would speak to me. It had been glued together and hollowed out, and inside was a little cell phone and charger.

I started laughing. "Whatcha got there?" Josh said.

"I don't have anything here, which is what you'll say if you value your reproductive organs," I said.

"I have seen nothing, sir," Josh said, smiling.

I put the phone under my pillow to muffle the sound and powered it up. A bunch of alert messages came through, and once the incriminating beeps had stopped, I pulled the phone out. "5 text messages" the screen said.

Message 1. From: Diana. *You're welcome. Unlimited texts. All our #s loaded in. Only 1k minutes for whole term, so use wisely.*

Message 2. From: Diana. *Oh yeah. Emmy has one too. Duh.*

Message 3. From: Diana. *Txt when you get this. We have a*

pool for how long it'll take you to figure out my hint.

Message 4: From: Chip. *Sorry, man. Gave you my save files & some anime by mistake. I have the porn.*

Oh well.

Message 5. From: Emmy. *Hey! Are you out there?*

This one was from three hours ago. I hoped she didn't think I was ignoring her or something. I quickly replied.

Hey! How are you!

I stared at the phone for a full five minutes, and just when I was ready to turn it off and put it back inside the Ass of Fire, it buzzed in my hand.

Better now.

Me too, I sent back.

So much to tell you! she sent.

Unlimited texts. :) I sent back, and then immediately wondered if the smiley face was too corny. Probably.

Got therapy in 10 min. she sent.

2nite after lites out? I sent back.

kk. I miss you.

I miss you too.

And she was gone. I sent a quick text to Diana to let her know it actually took me less than twenty-four hours to figure it out. And then I gathered up my books and walked out to go to my therapy appointment.

It was a beautiful day at Assland, and I felt something in the pit of my stomach that wasn't sour or cold. It was warming me up from the inside.

Because I had to be screwed up, I had to have a dad who was a tool, and I had to stay at Assland at least until the end of the term.

But I didn't have to be alone.

I guess that's about all anybody could ask for.

ACKNOWLEDGMENTS

THANKS TO BRENDAN HALPIN FOR THE FUNNY, DEEP, AND ALWAYS unexpected material to riff off of; big love to my mom and Team Cook–Steve-o, Courtney, Kelsey–for being the most loyal and hilarious crew anyone could ever wish for; cheers to my extended family, especially Tom, Sandy and brood, Nana and Papa, Jim and Samira, Aunt Ruth, and the Clingers for being so supportive; a round of applause to Holly Root for totally getting me and my kooky ideas; props to Greg Ferguson for seeing the potential in our work and making us dig even deeper to unearth a real jewel; a shout-out to the ever-talented, kind, and funny Rosie for being the inspiration behind Emmy; huge appreciation for Ashley and everyone at La Europa for saving us all; and unending gratitude to my amazing friends who lift me up and make me whole, including but not limited to Suzanne, Sue, Michele, Alison, Charlotte, two Heathers Lindas and Julies, Joanna, Lisa, Leslie, Carla, Amy, Jan, Aimee, Betsy, and Jackie. —*T.C.*

THANKS TO TRISH COOK FOR THE EXCELLENT IDEA AND FOR BEING fun to work with; thanks to Suzanne, Casey, Rowen, and Kylie for putting up with me; thanks to Doug Stewart for believing in me and my work for years; thanks to Greg Ferguson for helping us find the excellent book inside a somewhat ragged draft; thanks to Emily Franklin, Dan Waters, and Dana Reinhardt for ongoing moral support. —*B.H.*